F Jewell

Little Abe

Or, the Bishop of Berry Brow. Being the life of Abraham Lockwood

F Jewell

Little Abe
Or, the Bishop of Berry Brow. Being the life of Abraham Lockwood

ISBN/EAN: 9783337419622

Printed in Europe, USA, Canada, Australia, Japan

Cover: Foto ©Raphael Reischuk / pixelio.de

More available books at **www.hansebooks.com**

LITTLE ABE:

OR,

𝕿𝖍𝖊 𝕭𝖎𝖘𝖍𝖔𝖕 𝖔𝖋 𝕭𝖊𝖗𝖗𝖞 𝕭𝖗𝖔𝖜.

BEING THE LIFE OF

ABRAHAM LOCKWOOD,

A Quaint and Popular Yorkshire Local Preacher in the Methodist New Connexion.

BY

F. JEWELL.

EIGHTH THOUSAND.

LONDON:

PUBLISHED FOR THE PROPRIETOR,

T. WOOLMER, 2, CASTLE STREET, CITY ROAD, E.C ;

AND 66, PATERNOSTER ROW, E.C.

1884.

Abraham Pilling, Esq.,

ASTLEY BRIDGE,

BOLTON,

I DEDICATE TO YOU THIS RECORD OF THE

LIFE AND LABOURS OF ONE WHOSE WORTH YOU KNEW

AND APPRECIATED, AS A

MARK OF ESTEEM FOR YOUR ZEALOUS EXERTIONS

TO

ADVANCE THE KINGDOM OF CHRIST.

PREFACE.

I DESIRE to express my thanks to all those friends who have kindly assisted me in collecting materials for these pages; and I am especially indebted to my friends the Rev. T. D. Crothers and the Rev. W. J. Townsend for the cheerful services they have rendered me in preparing the little work for printing.

Whilst trying to give a faithful account of the life and character of Abraham Lockwood, I have done my best to make the narrative both readable and profitable; but I am sensible that there are many faults in the volume. Such as it is, however, I humbly offer it to the public, with the earnest prayer that it may prove a blessing to many.

F. JEWELL.

BETHEL VILLA,
HULL, 1880.

CONTENTS.

CHAPTER I.

PAGE

BIRTH AND PARENTAGE I

CHAPTER II.

EARLY INCIDENTS 7

CHAPTER III.

HIS CONVERSION 20

CHAPTER IV.

ABE A NEW CHARACTER IN THE VILLAGE . . 23

CHAPTER V.

IN MEMBERSHIP WITH THE CHURCH . . 36

CHAPTER VI.

"FOR BETTER, FOR WORSE" . . . 41

b

CHAPTER VII.

PAGE

WIND AND TIDE AGAINST 52

CHAPTER VIII.

THE CLOUDS BEGIN TO BREAK 59

CHAPTER IX.

SALEM CHAPEL 64

·CHAPTER X.

ABE BECOMES A LOCAL PREACHER . . . 70

CHAPTER XI.

IN PRACTICE 81

CHAPTER XII.

"BUTTERFLY PREACHERS" 85

CHAPTER XIII.

VARIOUS WAYS OUT OF DIFFICULTIES . . 91

CHAPTER XIV.

ABE'S TITLES AND TROUBLES 99

CHAPTER XV.

A BASKET OF FRAGMENTS . . . . 11.

CHAPTER XVI.

"I AM A WONDER UNTO MANY" . . . 121

CHAPTER XVII.

PAGE

ABE AS A CLASS LEADER 127

CHAPTER XVIII.

"WORKING OVERTIME" 136

CHAPTER XIX.

METHODIST LOVEFEAST 142

CHAPTER XX.

PATIENT IN TRIBULATION 153

CHAPTER XXI.

"THE LIBERAL DEVISETH LIBERAL THINGS" . . 163

CHAPTER XXII.

USED UP 173

CHAPTER XXIII.

"BETTER IS THE END OF A THING THAN THE
BEGINNING" 179

CHAPTER I.

Birth and Parentage.

ABRAHAM LOCKWOOD was born on the 3rd November, 1792. His birthplace, also called Lockwood, is situated about a mile and half out of Huddersfield.

It makes no pretensions to importance in any way. The only public building which it boasts, is the Mechanics' Institute, a structure of moderate size, yet substantially built. Its one main street is lined with some very excellent shops, some of whose owners, report says, have made a nice little competency there. It still boasts a toll-bar of its own, which is guarded on either side by two white wooden posts, that take the liberty of preventing all cattle, horses, and asses from evading the gate, and of unceremoniously squeezing into the narrowest limits every person who prefers pavement to the highroad. Lockwood is also important enough to receive the attention of two or three

'buses which ply to and fro between there and
Huddersfield, as well as to have the honour of a
railway station on the L. and Y. line. Of course
years ago, when Abraham Lockwood was brought
into the world, this locality was not so attractive
as it now is; only a few cottages straggled along
the level or up the hill towards Berry Brow, mostly
inhabited by weavers and others employed in the
cloth manufacture of the neighbourhood. Among
these humble cottages there stood, on what is
known as the Scarr, one even more unpretentious
than the rest: it boasted only one story and two
or three rooms in all; it was what Abe used to
call a " one-decker."

In this little hut dwelt the parents of Abe Lockwood; the fact of their residing in such a humble
home, shows sufficiently that they were poor,
perhaps poorer than their neighbours. However,
in that same single-storied cot in Lockwood, Abe
Lockwood was born, a Lockwoodite by double
right, and though age has seriously told upon its
appearance, it stands to this day. We sometimes see little old men living on, and year by
year growing less and less, until we begin to
speculate about the probable time it will require at
their rate of diminution for nothing to remain of
them; and the same may be said of the little old
house in which Abe Lockwood was born; it was
always little, but as years have slowly added to its
age, it has gradually begun to look less, and now,

as other houses of larger size and more improved style have sprung up all around the neighbourhood, it has shrunk into the most diminutive little hut that can well be imagined as a dwelling house, and it only requires time enough for it to be gone altogether.*

Abe's parents were a poor but honest pair, and laboured hard to make ends meet. William Lockwood, his father, was a cloth-dresser, and worked on Almondbury common, about a mile from his home, earning but a scanty living for the family. In those days, when machinery was almost unknown in the manufacture and finish of cloth, the men had to work harder and longer and earned much less than now. Those were the times when hard-working men thought that the introduction of machinery into cloth mills would take all the work out of their hands, and all the bread out of their mouths; and this was the very locality where the greatest hostility was shown by the people to such innovations. Many a threatened outbreak was heard of about that time, and in two or three instances the smouldering fire in the men's minds actually burst forth into riot and rising, when they found that the great masters were determined to have their own way and introduce machinery into their mills. Abe himself was led, some years after, to take part in one of these risings, and narrowly

* Since the above was written, this little cottage has been removed to afford room for a larger building.

escaped the hands of the law, while several others were lodged for some time in York jail in recognition of the part they had taken in the riots.

Abe's father was a quiet, moral-living man, whose chief aim for many years seemed to be to provide for his own household; but in after times his thoughts were drawn to things higher as well, and he became a God-fearing man; yet during Abe's early life, the most that can be said for his father is that he was an honest, hard-working, and well-disposed man.

His mother was a good Christian woman, and was for a long time a member with the Methodists in Huddersfield, and attended the old chapel which formerly stood on Chapel Hill. There is no doubt that the early teaching of his kind and pious mother had a great deal to do with the formation of Abe's Christian character in after years. Certainly a long time elapsed before there was any sign of spiritual life in her son; indeed, she was called away to her eternal rest before there was any indication of good in his heart; what matters that? the good seed was there; it would bide its time and then grow all the stronger. Sometimes people conclude that because there is not immediate growth there is no life; this does not follow; the grain may slumber for years, then wake up and grow rapidly. I on one occasion saved some orange pippins, dried and planted them with the hope that they might grow; as time went on, I

watered and watched them, but there was no indication of growth; months went by : I lost heart,
gave over watering, threw the plant-pot in which
they were sown out of doors ; a year was gone by
and more, when one day my eye fell on this same
pot all covered with green growth. "Hey! what's
this?" why, positively, they are young orange
plants, standing up hardy and healthy, protesting
against my want of faith and patience. It is often
the same with the growth of other seed in the
human breast; when parents have waited long in
vain, their faith grows gradually less and less, until
it dies out in despair ; but the good seed may not
die, it is sleeping, it lives its winter life, and then
under the tender and genial touch of some spring-
like influences it begins to grow. " Be not afraid,
only believe," said the Master of the vineyard.

Why the young baby that had come to reside
in that little cot should have the honourable name
of Abraham may be a subject of question by some.
It evidently was not to perpetuate his father's
name, though from the beginning of generations
this has been a sufficient argument for calling son
after father; on that ground John Baptist had a
narrow escape from being called Zacharias. That
however could not influence the decision in Abraham Lockwood's case, because his father's name
was William. Perhaps it was that the child indicated a patriarchal spirit, and conducted himself
like a *stranger in a strange land*, in which case

there might be a suggestion of that name. Perhaps it was a piece of parental forethought, for
knowing well that they could never confer riches
upon him, or place him in a position to make them
himself, they determined to do that for him, which
everyone must say is far better, they would see to
it that he had a *good name* among men, and so
they called him Abraham. This ancient and vene-
rable name, however, soon underwent a transfor-
mation, and appeared in the undignified form of
"Abe." The alteration at least exhibited a mark
of economy, even if it involved the sacrifice of
good taste ; there certainly was a saving of time
in saying " Abe " instead of " Abraham," which is
very important when things have to be done in a
hurry ; and then it may be that to some ears it
would sound more musical and familiar than the
full-length designation. Howbeit, there always
seemed a strange contrariness between Abe and
his name. When he was a baby they called him
by the antiquated name of " Abraham." As he
grew older and bigger, they shortened his name to
" Abe," and when he was a full-grown man, and
father of a family, he was commonly known as
" Little Abe." The name and the bearer seemed
to have started to run a circle in contrary directions, till they met exactly at the opposite point
in old age, when for the first time there was seen
the fitness between the man and his name, and he
was respectfully called " Abraham Lockwood."

CHAPTER II.

Early Incidents.

NOTHING particular is reported of his early life in that little home; there are no accounts of any hair-breadth escapes from being run over by cart-wheels, or of his being nearly burnt to death while playing with the kitchen fire, or of his straying away from home and taking to the adjacent woods, and the whole neighbourhood being out in quest of him, or that he even, during this interesting period of his history, either fell headlong into a coal-pit, or wandered out of his depth in the canal near by; there is, however, every probability, considering his lively disposition, that his mother had her time pretty well occupied in keeping him within bounds.

On reaching the notable age of six years, a very important change came over the even course of his young life. His parents sent him to work in a coal-pit; people in these days will scarcely credit

such a thing, but it is nevertheless true ; nor was
this an extraordinary case, for children of poor
parents were commonly sent to work in the pits at
that early age, when Abe was a child. The work
which they did was not difficult ; perhaps it might
be the opening or shutting of a door in one of the
drifts ; but whatever it was our hearts revolt at the
idea of sending a child of such tender years into a
coal mine, and thanks to the advance of civilization,
and an improved legislation on these things, such
an enormity would not now be permitted.

In some dark corner of that deep mine poor
little Abe was found day by day doing the work
assigned to him, and earning a trifle of wages which
helped to keep bread in the little home at Lockwood Scarr. He went out early in the morning,
and came home late at night, with the men who
wrought in the same pit, his little hands and feet
often benumbed with cold and wet, and he so tired
with his toils that many a time his poor mother
has had to lift him out of bed of a morning, and
put his little grimy suit of clothes on him, and send
him off with the rest almost before the child was
awake. Many a time he was so weary on coming
out of the pit that he has not been able to drag
himself along home, and some kind collier seeing
his tears has lifted him on his shoulder and carried
him, while he has slept there as soundly as if on a
bed of down.

Some few years passed on, during which time

Abe continued to work in the coal pit with but little change, except that as he grew older and stronger he was put to other work, and earned a better wage. His parents, however, were not satisfied that their son should live and die a collier, they thought him capable of something else; besides that, there were always the dangers associated with that calling in which so many were maimed or killed. They therefore determined that their son should be a mechanic, and learn to earn his bread above ground. After a while they found a master who was willing to take him into his employ and teach him his handicraft. It was customary in those days for a master to take the apprentice to live with him in his house, and find him in food and clothes. So Abe was given over to his new master, with the hope that he would do well for him, and the boy would turn out a good servant.

Now it is quite possible all this was done by the kind parents without consulting Abe's mind on the subject, which certainly had a good deal to do with the realization of their hopes, more perhaps than they thought; however they soon discovered it, for in a day or two Abe returned home with the information that he didn't like it, and should not be bound to any man. It was a sad disappointment to the honest pair, who had begun to indulge in expectations that some time "aar Abe may be mester hissen;" they however saw that it was of no use pressing him to go back, and so they com-

promised the matter by setting about to find him
another master. Abe was again despatched from
home with many a kind word of advice, and the
hope that he would mind his work, learn the trade,
and turn out to be a good man. But what was their
surprise and pain at the end of about a week to see
Abe walk into the house again with a bundle in
his hand. "Oh, Abe, my lad, what's brought thee
here so sooin? what's ta gotten in th' bundle?"
exclaimed his mother. "Why, gotten my things to
be sure; I couldn't leave them behind when I'm
going back no maar;" and sure enough he had
come home with the information as before, he
didn't like being bound to any man.

The probability is that there was something
in the kind of treatment Abe met with in both
those cases that helped to set his mind so much
against the life of an apprentice away from home.
All masters in those days were not particularly
kind in their manners towards apprentices: some
honourable exceptions could easily be found no
doubt, but as a rule, boys in such positions were
not very kindly used; hard work from early morning to late at night, hard fare at meal times, hard
cuffs between meals, and a hard bed with scanty
covering at nights,—it was no very enviable position for a youth to occupy, and certainly not one
to which a spirited lad would quietly submit. It
may be that Abe, during the short probations he
had served at these two places, had learnt too

much of the ways of the establishments for so young a hireling, and found they would not suit his peculiar tastes, and therefore he decided twice over to return home, bringing his bundle of clothes without giving any explanations or notice to any one.

Be that as it may, here he was at home again a second time, much to the annoyance of his father, who was bent upon the lad learning some handicraft. Abe remained at home a short time, when one day his father told him he had got another place for him, with an excellent man, who would take him a little while on trial, and if they liked each other he might then be indentured. His father had been at some trouble to find a master farther away from home, in the hope that when once Abe was a good way off he might be induced to stay ; in this he was acting on the principle that the power of attraction is weakened by a wider radius, which may be correct when applied to some things, but not to all. This new master lived in Lancashire, and thither young Abraham was sent in due course. A month or so passed away, and all seemed to promise a satisfactory arrangement, until one morning Abe heard a conversation in the family, from which he gathered that his master was going to Marsden, where he expected to meet Mr. Lockwood at a certain inn, and make final arrangements for Abe's apprenticeship. This opened the old sore ; Abe

couldn't rest : " he wouldn't stay, that he wouldn't,
he would be off home ; " but how was he to get
there ? he didn't know the way, and thirty miles
or more was a long journey in those days. He
determined therefore to keep his eye on his master
until he saw him off for Marsden, which was more
than half the distance to his home, and then he
set away after him on the same road, never losing
sight of him for one minute. On they went mile
after mile along the roads until they reached
Marsden, where he saw his master enter the inn.
Now Abe had to pass in front of this very house,
but he didn't want to be discovered, so he adroitly
turned up his coat collar over the side of his face,
and pulled down his cap, and set off running as
fast as he could, and just as he was passing the
inn he took one hurried look from under his mask,
and there, in the open window, he saw two men
side by side, his master and his father. Of course
he concluded they must have seen him, and would
be out immediately to fetch him back ; this idea
only lent speed to his weary feet, so that he ran
faster than ever on through the solitary street of
the old village, away out on the road, never turning
to look behind, lest he might see all Marsden
coming in pursuit of him. Exhausted nature however at length compelled him to slacken his pace,
and on turning to look back he found he had only
been pursued by his own fears. The two men sat
still in the inn, talking over and settling the terms

of the apprenticeship, fixing the time when the indenture should be signed and the boy bound to his new master. Each of them took his journey homeward ; neither of them was prepared for what awaited him. One of them found on arriving home that Abe had gone, and the other discovered the very opposite, that he had come, and both were alike vexed.

It is likely that poor Abe would have had to trot back again the next day if his mother had not taken his part. Dear woman, she had been a whole month without seeing her boy, and many an anxious thought had she about him during that period ; many a time when her fond heart yearned for him, she had well nigh said she wished they had never sent him away; many a time when some foot had been heard at the door her heart stopped at the thought, that it might be him ; and now that he had come, really come, had run so far to be near her, had come so weary, footsore, and hungry, had laid his weary head on the end of the table and wept tears of trouble and pleasure, had fallen asleep there as he sat, she put her kind arms around him, kissed his hot forehead and said, "Dear lad, they shall not take him away from his mother any more for all the masters and trades in the land." So it was of no use that Mr. Lockwood should argue for his going back ; he had to yield inevitably, for what man can think to contend long against his *better* half? From that time all attempt to bring Abraham up as an artificer ended, and he found employment with his father as a cloth-finisher, at which he worked most of his lifetime afterwards.

Soon after these stirring little events had gone by, another happened in that household which brought far more pain and anxiety than anything that had preceded it. The youth who would not be parted from his mother, could not prevent his mother from leaving him, and the separation took place; death stept in, and without regard to the fond feelings which bound that little household together, bore away the wife and mother to the spirit land, while her body was laid among the dust of others in the yard of the old brick chapel in Chapel Hill, Huddersfield.

What a gap it made in that house! in the hearts of its inmates it left an open wound which only long months of patient endurance could heal. When a mother's dust is carried out and laid in the grave, it is the light of the domestic hearth gone out; it is the sweetest string gone from the family harp; that bereavement is like the breath of winter among tender flowers; the live tree around which entwined tender creepers is torn up, and they lie entangled on the ground, disconsolate and helpless, until the Great Father of us all shall give them strength to stand alone.

Abraham Lockwood's mother was dead, and a kind restraining hand, which many a time kept his wild and wayward spirit in subjection, was thereby withdrawn, and the ill effects in time began to show themselves in his conduct. As he grew older, and the trouble consequent on the loss of his mother wore off, Abe gradually associated with evil companions, fell into their habits, until he became a wild and wicked young man. He never sank into those low habits of which some are guilty, who neglect the appearance and cleanliness of their own person, and go about on Sundays and weekdays unwashed and in their working attire. Abe had more respect for himself, and was always looked upon among his friends as a dandy. I have heard old people say he was a proud young man, and withal of a very sprightly appearance.

Abe took great pride in his personal appearance, and when not in his working clothes he usually wore a blue coat in the old dress style, such as "Father Taylor" would call "a gaf-topsail jacket." There were the usual and attractive brass buttons to the coat, drab knee-breeches, blue stockings, low tied shoes with buckles ; and really everyone who knew Abe thought he was a proud young man. Perhaps he was, but it is not always an indication of pride when young people bestow more care upon their appearance than do their fellows ; it may arise from a desire to appear respectable and be respected. No one will think I am trying to extenuate the foolish and extravagant love of dress which some people show, who adorn themselves in silks or broadcloth, for which they have to go into debt without the means of paying. Some are most unsparing in the way they lavish money on their own persons, but only ask them to bestow something on a charitable institution, or on the cause of God, and how poor they are; how careful not to be guilty of the sin of *extravagance;* how anxious not to be *generous before being just.*

There is a propriety which ought to be observed with regard to dress as well as other things, and it will commend itself to the judgment as well as to the eye. Some young people are the very opposite to Abe; they bestow scanty attentions on their appearance,—how can they think that any one else will pay them any regard? Their appearance is like the index to a book; you see in a minute what the work contains, and so you may generally form a correct idea of the character of an individual by his habitual personal appearance. "Character shows through," is a good saying, and would make a profitable study for most of us; it shows through the skin, the dress, the manners, the speech, through everything; people ought to remember this, and it would have a good influence on their conduct.

A few years after his mother's death his father married again, and removed about a mile further up the hill, to a place called Berry Brow. This village is situated about two miles out of Hudders-field, and is the notable place where "little Abe"

spent the greater part of his days. It stands on
the brow of a hill which bounds one side of the
wealthy and picturesque valley that winds along
from Huddersfield to Penistone. It boasts one
main street, which sidles along down the hill-side
with here and there a clever curve, just enough to
prevent you from taking a full-length view of the
street; on and down it goes, the houses on the one
side looking down on those opposite, and evidently
having the advantages of being higher up in the
world than their neighbours, until it terminates in
the highroad leading out of the village towards
Honley and Penistone.

Run your eye down over the breast of the hill,
and you have a delightful landscape picture, com-
prising almost everything which an artist would
deem desirable for an effective painting, *and a
little to spare.* There, nearly at the bottom of the
gradient, stands the handsome old village church,
with its tower and pinnacles, reaching up among
the tall trees; and around it, a consecrated en-
closure, guarding the monuments of the dead,
which are mingled with melancholy shrubs, planted
there by hands of mourners whose memories of
the departed are fitly symbolized by those per-
petual evergreens. On this side and beyond the
sleeping graveyard, on either arm, are scattered, in
pretty confusion, the houses of those who have
retired from the main street for the sake of a little
garden plot or other convenience. Now there is

2

some pretence at a terrace, numbering two or three
dwellings ; then an abrupt break, and houses stand
independent and alone as if quietly contemplating
the lovely scenery of valley, hill, and forest, which
are visible from that spot. Down there in the
bottom of the valley, stand those mighty many-
windowed cloth mills, whose great flat, unspeak-
able faces, seem to be covered all over with
spectacles, out of which they can look for ever
without winking ; there the men, women, and
children, born and bred in the hills, find honest
toil with which to win bread and comforts ; while
with a twisting course there runs along the wealthy
dale a little river, from which these giant mills
suck up their daily drink. Across the narrow
valley and you are into a dense woody growth,
which climbs the hills to their very crown, and
sweeps away, mingling with the sky.

To this village the Lockwood family removed ;
and coming more directly under religious influences,
the father very soon became converted, and united
with the Methodist Church, along with his wife.
This had a great influence on Abe for good ; he
began to attend the Sunday-school, which was
conducted in a room, in what was called the Steps
Mill, on the road between Berry Brow and Honley.
This was Abe's college ; here he began, and here
he finished his education ; no other school did he
ever attend ; and for what little knowledge he had,
he was indebted to the kindness of those who

taught in that school; yet all he learnt here was to *read. Writing* was a branch of study which Abe thought altogether beyond his power ; many times he endeavoured to learn the mysterious art, but after struggling on as far as the stage of pot-hooks and crooks, he gave up in disgust, and never tried again. He used to say he firmly believed the Lord never meant him to be a writer, or he would have given him a talent for it. Now in this Abe was certainly labouring under a false impression, and underrating his own ability; he was as well able to learn the art of writing as many others in similar circumstances. . How many persons hav we known who have grown up to manhood and womanhood, before they knew one letter from another, and yet they have commenced to learn, and persevered in the work, until they have attained at least a moderate proficiency, and some even more than that. What Abe lacked more than talent, was a determination to learn ; for if he had been resolved, he could have become a good pen-man as well as others ; in this he was to blame, whether he thought so or not. Education can only be had by those who will work for it, and considering its immense value to every person, all who neglect it are blameworthy, and must pay the penalties, as Abe did all through his life.

CHAPTER III.

His Conversion.

PEOPLE talk of great changes in life, and point to periods and events which seem to have turned their whole course into a different channel ; but there is nothing that can happen to any individual which will make such an alteration in his life as *conversion*. Thousands of persons who had been almost useless in the world, after that event have become valuable members of society ; others who have neglected and abused their talents and opportunities, have become thoughtful and diligent ; others who have lived in riot and sin, wasting the energies of body and mind, have learnt to live at peace with all men, and walk in the fear of God and hope of heaven. Having become new creatures, they have shown it in every line of their conduct. "Old things have passed away, and behold, all things have become new."

It was never more strikingly illustrated than in

the case of Abraham Lockwood. For a length of
time after he had begun to attend Sunday-school,
there was a manifest difference in Abe's manner.
Not that he was really living a better life, for he
was just as sinful as before, only he was *not now
thoughtless;* he might go to the ale-house with his
associates, but he went home to think about it
after ; he might swear and laugh like the rest of
them when they were together, but he was no
sooner alone than he felt the stings of a remorseful
conscience; he was gradually getting into that
state when a man dreads to be alone with himself ;
there was always something speaking to him from
within, and the voice was getting stronger and
stronger every week, till sometimes it fairly startled
him, and made him afraid ; often he would try to
run away from it, but it was of no use ; the moment
he stopped, panting from the exertion, it was there
again ; many a time he tried to deaden the voice
in the deafening noise of the mill, but the more
he endeavoured to destroy it, by some mysterious
contradiction, the more intently he found himself
listening for it ; it spoilt all the pleasures of sin by
its presence ; it was with him night and day ; it
followed him in his sleep, and was waiting for him
when he awoke ; it made him miserable. Poor Abe
was *under conviction of sin ;* he was tasting the
wormwood of a guilty conscience, than which
nothing is more dreadful, and nothing is more
hopeful, because it is the bitter that oft worketh

itself sweet; it was so with Abe. While he was
in this state of mind, the Rev. David Stoner came
to preach in the Wesleyan Chapel at Almondbury.
His fame drew many to hear him, and among the
rest Abraham Lockwood. He went partly out of
curiosity, and partly in the hope of getting relief
to his mind; however, he only came away worse
than before; he was miserable, and it now began
to show itself to his companions. " Pain will out,"
like murder. " What's the matter, Abe ? " they
would say to him. " Oh, nothing particular," he
would reply. And then among themselves they said,
" Abe looks very queer, he's ill ; " then they tried
to enliven him. " Come, cheer up, old boy, we'll
have a yarn." One would tell some droll tale, and
another would say something comical in order to
make him laugh ; and laugh he did, he must laugh ;
it would never do to let those fellows know what
was passing in his mind ; so he laughed loud as
any of them, but what a laugh !—how empty and
hollow, how joyless and unreal, how unlike his
former bursts of feeling !—a got-up laugh, which
showed plainer than ever *something was wrong.*
Abe knew it, and he felt it was of no use trying
any longer to keep up a sham happiness, and all
the time be in torments from a guilty conscience ;
he therefore resolved to give up sin and lead a new
life. He probably was hastened to that decision
by a remark which fell from his father's lips ; the
old man had noticed for some time that Abe was

not in his usual spirits. He would come home of
an evening and sit looking into the fire for an hour
without speaking or moving ; he had given over
singing in the house, and he seemed as if he hadn't
spirit enough left to whistle to the little bird in the
cage; his meals lay almost untasted, and his tea
would go cold before he had taken any.

" Come, my lad, thaa mun get thee tea thaa
knows," said the old father one evening.

" Yes," said Abe, as he pretended to push something into his mouth.

" What's matter with th' ? " the father inquired;
" thaa's not like theesen, nor hasn't been for mony
a week."

Abe's eyes grew moist, and his chin trembled,
but he called himself to order, no babyism now.

The old man, still looking at him, and keen
enough to notice the struggle he had to master
his feelings, went on to say, " Thaa's poorly, my
lad, thaa mun goa to th' doctor, and see if he
canna gie thee some'at."

" No earthly doctor can do onything for me,"
answered Abe ; " it's th' Physician of souls that I
want. Oh, father, I am unhappy; my sins are
troubling me noight and day; I don't know what
will become of me : *I feel like lost.*"

" My poor lad, the Lord have mercy on thee,'
replied the old man, as Abe put on his cap and
walked hurriedly out of the house. He went out
scarcely knowing why; perhaps to hide his trouble

from his dear old father; perhaps to smother his emotions, which were rapidly gaining the mastery over him, or maybe he knew not why,—an impulse was upon him, and it carried him forth into the cool evening air; away he went at a brisk walk from the village in the direction of Almondbury common. Faster and faster he went, faster and faster as if to keep up with the rapid current of his thoughts; the distance was uncounted, the direction unheeded, the time forgotten; one thought only occupied his tempest-torn mind, what must he do to be saved! There are some who would think him very foolish to give himself so much concern on a matter of that sort; but the fact is, Abe was just beginning to act the part of a wise man in renouncing his old habits and declaring for Christ. No human eye followed him on that lonely walk to the common, and no human friend accompanied him; he was alone, the thought pleased him; he looked around all over the face of the common, but no person was visible. *Abe was alone with God*, and he determined to speak to Him, and tell Him all his burden of sorrow. Near to where he stood, there was a large tree growing, whose lofty branches were uplifted to heaven; it stood just at the bottom of a little grassy slope of four or five yards deep, and close to the side of a small clear stream of water, which ran gurgling and rippling along, moistening the great roots of this tree; it was here, under its spreading boughs and gnarled trunk, *Abe found a place for prayer.* Down on his knees he cast himself, and his first utterance consecrated that spot as a closet, " God be merciful to me a sinner ! " He only needed to utter the first cry, others followed in rapid and earnest succession, till all the restraints upon his soul were broken asunder, and in an agony he wrestled for salvation. Hour after hour fled by ; twilight gave place to darkness ; lights shone from the cottage windows away on the hill-sides ; distant watch-dogs answered each other's unwearying bark ; neighbours in the village yonder, stood chatting by their open doors in the quiet night, and in many a cottage home hard by, children and grown-up men sat quietly eating their last meal before retiring to bed : but none of them knew that out on Almondbury common, at the foot of a great rude tree, a man, one of their neighbours, a sinner like themselves, *was praying.* No, no, they didn't know : there is many a thing goes on of vital interest to us, which even our nearest friends know nothing about ; but there are other eyes, invisible, which look down upon us from their starry heights seeing all our ways. So they looked, while Abe wrestled for liberty. His chief snare at this time was, that he was *too bad for Christ to save ;* it was a terrible thought to him, and had so much of seeming truth in it, that he at times almost despaired ; then again he remembered that he could not be too bad for

Christ to save; no, HE could save to the very uttermost all that came unto Him; Abe tried to believe that with all his heart, and as he struggled against his doubts and fears, faith grew stronger and bolder, then in a moment the snare broke, the dark cloud over his soul burst, and out from the cleft there came a voice, which thrilled his whole being. "Arise, shine; for thy light is come, and the glory of the Lord is risen upon thee." "Glory! Glory!! Glory!!!" burst from his enraptured lips; his "light was come,"—what a light! a soul full, *full* of the light of Divine smiles. No wonder Abe forgot everything else, in the joys of that ecstatic moment. He leaped, laughed, wept, shouted the praises of God till his voice might have been heard far away over the waste, as he turned his steps towards home that night. "Why, he's made a bron new man o' me. I hardly know mysen. Hallelujah!"

He was not long in reaching home, nor long in letting them know, when he got there, what a change had come over him. In he went, with a face shining in all the brightness of his new-found joy. "He's made a bron new man o' me! He's made a bron new man o' me. Hallelujah! Hallelujah!"

The change in his whole manner and appearance was so great, that his poor old father was at first alarmed lest he had gone wrong in his mind; but Abe assured him he had just got right, and by God's help he meant to keep so.

Oh, if Abe had just got right by the wonderful change which God had wrought in him, (and who can doubt it ?) how many there are in the world *who are all wrong,* living the wrong life, striving for the wrong things, going the wrong way, and running towards the wrong goal ! Oh, how many are spending this short life in the pursuit of things which are worthless and worse; sacrificing their souls' best interests for the brief indulgence of sinful tastes, or spending the rapidly accumulating years of their life in dark indifference to eternal things !

The escape of one such sinner as Abe from the captivity in which the ungodly are all held, may for a brief hour excite remark, perhaps a desire for liberty, too, in the minds of some others; but these good desires are often only of short duration, they die where they were born, and almost as soon, and the soul returns to its former state ; the sleeper slumbers on ; the drunkard drinks harder ; the swearer blasphemes more fiercely ; the libertine indulges in greater excesses ; and all these hordes of ungodly men push on again down the broad and easy incline to the pit of Hell. Do people know that the end of a sinful life is Hell ? Do people believe ? Why, then, do they press their way down to such a place ?

CHAPTER IV.

Abe a New Character in the Village.

"HAST ta yeard th' news?" said one neighbour to another, on the morning following the happy event narrated in the preceding chapter.

"What news dost ta mean?"

"Aye well, thaa has'n't yeard what happened last noight; doan't look so scared, mon; th' mill worn't burnt daan; nor th' river droid up; nor Amebury (Almondbury) common transported; but some'at stranger nor that."

"Why, whatever dost ta mean?"

"I mean that Abe Lockwood's been and gotton converted last noight, and he's up and off to his wark this morning, shaating and singing like a madman."

"Abe Lockwood converted!" replied the other in astonishment, and pausing between each word, as if to realize his own sayings. "Nay,—I'll niver believe that."

" It's as true as thaa and me is here ; his father
telled me he wor aat hoalf at noight on Amebury
common, crying and praying by a big tree roit,
and he gat converted there all alone ; and when he
came into th' haase, his face was shining like th'
moonloight."

Here was news for the people of Berry Brow,
and how it flew from mouth to mouth, and from
house to house, till, before many hours, almost
every person in the village knew of the wonderful
change which had come over Abe. Some doubted
the report,—"It canna be soa," said one; another
" would sooiner think of ony one than him ; he's
making game on't, I'll lay onything." Others
thought, " If he's turned religious, it's no matter ;
he'll be as wild as iver by th' week-end." It was
out of all character for Abe Lockwood to be anything else than he had been, a rollicksome, laughing, drinking, ungodly young man.

How often people talk in this way, when they
hear of some giving their hearts to God ; " They
won't stand long ; give them a month, and it will
be all over," and such like injudicious things are
said even by some who ought to have more discretion. People talk without thinking, or make such
statements to cover their own shortcomings and
faults. Why shall they not stand ? are they in the
keeping of a feeble or fickle Saviour ? isn't His
grace as strong as sin ? is not Jesus always mightier
than the devil ? and have not millions of the

greatest sinners who have found the Lord, stood firm against the snares of the world, and all the devices of the wicked one? "He won't stand," is an old lie, which every young believer must set at defiance. "Stand fast, therefore, in the liberty wherewith Christ hath made us free, and be not entangled again with the yoke of bondage."

"Weant I stand," said Abe, "then I'll fall, but it shall be at the feet of Jesus." Ah, that is the best way to stand; fall at the feet of Jesus. It may seem a paradox in terms, but it is not in truth; it is on the Apostolic principle, "When I'm weak, then am I strong." So poor Abe laid himself down in order that he might not fall, and this is a plan which others might try in times of spiritual peril, and so escape the danger of backsliding.

Among others who canvassed the subject of his conversion were his old companions. One had gone out from among them that they were sorry to lose; he was such a merry fellow; his face was always sunny; his comical sayings had filled the public-house with roars of laughter many a time; he could sing a song better than any of them, and he was always ready; he was open-handed with his money whenever he had any; and indeed, he possessed most of the qualities which make a man a favourite among boon companions. His going out left a blank which was more felt than seen; a vacant seat in a public-house is soon filled; so if Abe was not there to occupy his own place some-

one else was ; but no matter who of his old associates were present, everyone *felt* Abe was absent,
and couldn't help showing it in some way.

They had all observed that he had not been
exactly himself lately ; "a little down in the
mouth," and very quiet at times ; but never divin-
ing the reason, they had put it down to the wrong
cause, or thought very little about it ; and then
Abe had so often roused himself out of these
moods of mental abstraction by taking "another
glass," and having another song, that he had kept
his companions completely ignorant of the work
which was going on in his mind. So now it burst
upon them like a gun-shot ; they were amazed ;
but the devil seldom deserts his victims at a time
like that ; it would not be safe, he might lose some
more of them ; he comes to their help and counsels
them as to their conduct. "Well," says one of
them as they gathered in their usual place of resort
one night, " I s'pose Abe Lockwood will be gone
to prayer-meeting to sing Psalms with the old
women," at which the whole company burst into a
loud laugh at Abe's expense, and yet it cost him
nothing, which was more than any of them could
say of the drink they consumed that night.

Abe Lockwood had left them,—he was a changed
man; he had been converted on Amebury common ;
he had turned off into an entirely different course
from theirs ; he was a better man than any of
them : many such thoughts as these would obtrude

themselves on the minds of his former friends, and linger there in spite of all their efforts to keep clear of them.

Some time elapsed before any of these old associates were brought into immediate contact with Abe; whether they purposely kept out of his way, or he out of theirs, is not easy to say; perhaps both would be correct. He no doubt felt safest and happiest away from his old companions and everything which reminded him of them; they, too, had a misgiving that whenever they did meet Abe, he would say something that might make them uncomfortable; for they knew he would not beat about the bush, he would tell them his mind about their ways: so on the whole it was best to keep out of his way as long as they could.

Meanwhile, Abe was gathering strength day by day, for he was living in the constant spirit of prayer, which is the way to be strong. Night after night, a lone man might be seen kneeling at the root of a great tree on Almondbury common, pouring out his soul in prayer to God, until that spot became to the new convert the very gate of heaven; and for long years after, when Abe was established in the faith, he still frequently found his way there to pray; during the whole of his subsequent life, he never passed that spot without turning aside to hear what the Lord would say to him. Many of the most delightful times he ever had were experienced at the foot of that tree; and a visit there, where he breathed the native air of his spiritual life, invariably brought the glow of religious health to his soul.

As weeks and months went by, the people of Berry Brow became used to the fact of Abe Lockwood's conversion, and it ceased to excite any particular remark, except such as might pass between neighbours on seeing him go by.

"Aye, mun, what a change is in yon lad," one would say.

"You are roight naa," would be the response.

"He wor as big a rake as ony i' th' parish a few months sin'; I'd never ha' thowt o' Abe Lockwood turning religious."

"No, nor me noather, but we niver know what 'll come to us."

"No,—gooid-noight."

One day Abe and a former companion of his met full in front; there was no sliding away on either side,—they must speak. Both of them experienced a slight nervousness at first, but Abe plucked up courage and came boldly on.

"Naa, lad, haa art ta?"

"Oh, why, middling like, haa's yersen?"

"Aye, mun," said Abe, "it gets better and better, religion is th' best thing i' th' world; it's made me th' happiest chap i' Berry Braa."

"Why, thaa looks merry," said his companion.

"I is merry, and only wish thaa wor like me," and then Abe went on in his own simple, earnest,

3

and homely manner to preach Jesus to his friend ;
and before they parted, the man had proof enough
that Abe had found a better way of living than
his former one.

Many a time, as weeks and months rolled by, he
was thrown for a short time into company with
one or another of his old yoke-fellows in sin; and
often did they endeavour to lead him back again
into the ways and haunts he had forsaken ; but no,
no, he was not to be moved out of the new path
which he had taken for time and for eternity.

Abe was a very plain-spoken man, and sometimes used phrases which were anything but
refined, but this was compensated for by their
good sense.   Sometimes, when Satan was tempting
him to give up his religion, and return again into
the ways of sin, he would exclaim, "What ! give
up my blessed religion and return to thy swill-tub
agean ; I should be a great fooil to do that,—does
th' want to mak' me like an owd saa (sow), that's
been weshed, and then runs back into t' muck
agean ; nay, thaa's rolled me i' sin lang enough ;
I'm thankful to be aat o' thy mud-hoil, and by the
help of God, thaa'll get me there no maar."   Then
perhaps, when in conversation with some uncon-
verted neighbour on the all-absorbing theme of
religion, he would break out, "Aye, mun, yoa
doan't know haa grand it feels being weshed,
weshed i' th' blood of th' Lamb.   I wor that mucky,
all th' watter i' Holmfirth dam couldn't mak' me

daacent, but a drop of HIS blood did it in a moment. Glory to God ! "

Ah ! the precious blood of Jesus can make the foulest clean ; no matter how long or how deep sin has reigned in his heart, Jesus is able to remove it entirely, and bring in His grace and peace. He is a wonderful Physician, there is none like Him ; He has never been baffled yet, though for nearly two thousand years He has been called to exercise His power on the outcasts and incurables of our race. He knows the disease with which every poor sinner is afflicted, and He also understands the cure ; sinners who have long been given up by themselves, and others as well—poor, abandoned things, who have been kicked out of all orderly society, and left to rot in the moral filth of the streets, or die in the sewers of iniquity, have been found by Him, lifted out of the mire, washed in the streams of His grace, clothed in His righteousness, and made fit to sit among princes.

> " Jesus, Thy blood and righteousness
> My beauty are, my glorious dress ;
> 'Midst flaming worlds, in these arrayed,
> With joy shall I lift up my head."

CHAPTER V.

In Membership with the Church.

AS soon as Abe Lockwood found the Lord, he felt it was his duty and privilege to unite himseif with the people of God, and he therefore lost no time in seeking membership.

THE METHODIST NEW CONNEXION at that time had no chapel in Berry Brow, but conducted prayer-meetings, and held a weekly class in a cottage somewhere in the village. Abe knew these humble, earnest people, and felt drawn towards them by strong sympathy; he was sure he could feel at home among them, and they would be of very great assistance to him in building up his Christian character. What made him all the more willing to throw in his lot among them, was the fact that some of them had frequently shown an interest in his spiritual welfare before he became converted, and had endeavoured to induce him to attend their meetings; and now when they all knew the change that had taken place in him, they were the first to go after him and offer him the right hand of fellowship,—so he at once united himself heart and hand to their little band.

It would be well if that zeal and watching for souls, which characterized the early Methodists, were more frequently displayed among their successors ; how many who are now merely hovering outside the Christian Church, afraid to run after the pleasures of sin, ashamed to avow themselves in quest of salvation, would be brought to decision, and enabled to lead a happy and useful life. .

There are many thus hanging on the skirts of almost every Church, waiting to be gathered up, and shame on the members who quietly and indifferently permit this ! It must not be ; men's souls are too precious to be trifled with ; they have *cost too much* for us to allow them to starve and die on our doorstep ; open the door, put forth your hand, draw them kindly, but firmly, into the family of the Lord ; few of them will have heart to resist such efforts to save them ; but if they do, then go out to them, stay with them, persuade and entreat them, pray for them, pray on and on, and in the end you will prevail. We want more of this watching and waiting for souls in Churches; may God lay these souls on our hearts !

Abe became a member of the Methodist New Connexion in Berry Brow when it could scarcely be considered a Church, inasmuch as neither Christian sacrament nor preaching services were

established there : it was merely a class belonging
to the society in Huddersfield. That class, however, was the living germ out of which was in due
time developed a strong and flourishing Church,
having now a commodious chapel, and also an
excellent Sunday School, in which are growing
up hundreds of interesting children, who will some
day be a blessing to the neighbourhood, and an
honour to the Church of Christ.

To this little band of disciples our friend Abe
was a most valuable addition ; not that either then
or afterwards he brought them wealth, for he was
always poor, but because he contributed a zealous,
praying spirit, and encouraged the little flock to
fresh exertions.

He was no sooner admitted among them, than
he began to exercise his talents in prayer-meetings,
and although he sometimes got confused in his
utterances, he didn't care much, for he used to say,
" Th' Lord knows what I mean, and He can soort
th' words, and put 'em in their roight places ; bless
Him, He can read upsoide daan, or insoide aat."
But time and constant exercise made a wonderful
improvement in this respect, and as Abe felt less
difficulty in uttering what he meant, he also experienced less restraint of spirits, and began to show
himself in his own peculiar style.

He had a way of responding to almost everything that was prayed for, and interlacing remarks,
and sometimes explanations, when he thought them

necessary. Possibly these comments were more to himself than for any one else, and were often made quite unconsciously—a kind of thinking aloud. A rather amusing instance is given where Abe's notes of explanation were called forth. It appears that one night the weekly prayer-meeting was conducted as usual in the cottage of one of the members. Abe was there among a number of others, and they were having a very lively time together. As one after another engaged in earnest intercession at the throne of grace, the feelings of all present became very elevated, and they shouted for joy. At length, while one brother was praying, another got so happy that he could remain on his knees no longer. Springing to his feet, therefore, he began to jump, and in one of his upward move- ments he brought his head into sudden and violent contact with a basket of apples, which hung by a nail to the ceiling ; the basket oscillated a time or two, then slipped over the head of the nail, and spilt its contents on the head of the man that was praying. This singular event was deemed by him a sufficient reason for suspending his exercises, and opening his eyes to ascertain the cause. As soon as Abe observed the suspension of prayer, he exclaimed, " Pray on, lad ! it's nobbut th' owd woman's apple-cart upset," on receiving which timely exposition of the state of things, the good man resumed his intercessions, and the meeting returned to its former happy flow of feeling.

The time came when Abe was looked upon as
the life and soul of these little meetings: his
quaint sayings, his earnest prayers, his happy
experience, always animated and strengthened
those who were present, and made the meetings
real means of grace.   Then Abe was always there ;
he could be relied upon whoever might fail, so
that they all began to depend upon him, look to
him, and follow him, till, almost without knowing
it, he had become greatly responsible for the spiritual life of the little flock in Berry Brow, and
mainly instrumental in laying the foundations of
the cause there, which has now grown to very
interesting and influential proportions.

CHAPTER VI.

"For Better, for Worse."

MARRIAGE is a most important step in the life of any person ; happiness or misery in this world depend on it far more than many young people think. Nothing demands more careful thought, discrimination, and prayer, than the choice of a life partner. Especially professors of religion should consider this, lest they be tempted to break the apostolic injunction, and become "unequally yoked together with unbelievers."

It is painful to see how little regard is paid to this subject by some who profess to be disciples of Jesus, and yet allow their affections to be centred upon someone of the world. Pleased by an attractive appearance, winning manners, or something else of this kind, they are beguiled away beyond the line of demarcation which divides the church from the world, until, by-and-bye, they consummate a union of the flesh, where there cannot be a union of spirit, and light and darkness make a poor attempt to dwell together.

Self-deception is a very easy thing in matters of this sort; it is seldom difficult to find arguments in favour of that which the heart is set upon. The one that knows the Lord, will pray until the other is brought to him; neither will be guilty of casting the slightest hindrance in the way of the other, etc., etc., but how often have these pretty delusive devices been cast to the winds, or broken to atoms like glass toys in after life, and their framers made to pay the bitter penalties of disappointment, regret, and even backsliding for their early transgressions? The selection of a husband or wife is not a question of mere sentiment or feeling, but one which involves an important principle. In making it, we should take God into our counsel, and abide by His decisions. A young man who was a member in one of our churches once opened his mind to me on this subject; he very much admired a young person whom he mentioned; he said he had been praying about marriage with her for some time, and had left it entirely with the Lord, but said he, "I must have her, come what may." Prayer with submission like that is only a solemn mockery, and is sure to meet with its deserved reward. If we ask God to guide us, we must permit Him to lead; and whether the outcome suit our feelings or not, we may rest assured it will be for our ultimate welfare.

In the choice of his wife Abe Lockwood was wisely led, as a long and happy life together afterwards proved. It appears that soon after his conversion, Abe, who was always fond of singing, joined the choir of the Huddersfield Chapel. That was the age before organs were thought of in Methodist places of worship; other musical instruments obtained in those good old times : fiddles and bass viols, clarionets, flutes, hautboys, cornets, trombones, bassoons and serpents, delighted the ears and stirred the souls of our forefathers with their sacred harmony. Grand old times those were too; there was some scope for the musical genius and taste of men in those days, when if a man could not manipulate the keys and evoke the religious tones of a clarionet, he might vent his zeal in the trombone, or make melody on a triangle; then, the orchestra was a kind of safety valve, where zealous men might exert their powers until they were bathed in perspiration and exhausted. In those days the musicians were men of considerable influence in the public services; they could any time keep the congregation waiting while they tuned up to harmony, or while the first fiddle mended his string, or rosined his stick. True, a little accident would occasionally happen in the midst of the service, such as the falling of a bridge, but nobody was hurt, it was only a fiddle-bridge ; a nervous preacher might be just a little startled by the thwack behind him, and a few of the light sleepers might be suddenly aroused from their deep meditations to venture an inappropriate response; and other little matters might occasionally happen, as when some conspicuous instrument became excited, and played somewhat sharper than the others in the band, thereby giving a twinge of neuralgia to a few sensitive persons in the congregation; but then they shouldn't be so sensitive,—others were not, not even the musicians, and why should they? Besides, all these things, and a great many more, too numerous to mention, helped to throw some variety and feeling into the proceedings, and frequently afforded matter for lively conversation when the people came out of chapel. Can any one wonder, therefore, that the musical taste of the past should steadfastly resist every effort to bring about a change in the composition and conduct of our chapel orchestras?

Abe lived and flourished as a singer in those good old days, and it was one of his greatest enjoyments to take his place among the singers in the old High Street Chapel, and raise his alto voice in honour of Him "whose praise can ne'er be told."

But there was another little pleasure which Abe very much enjoyed after the services, and that was to walk home in company with a young woman, one of the singers, too, named Sarah Bradley. She lived at Berry Brow, and was a member in the same class as himself; she was about his own

age, and while she made no pretensions to beauty,
she was what the neighbours called "a real
bonny lass." Abe thought her the nicest and
handsomest young woman he ever gazed upon.
She was the very light of his eyes, and her conversation was real music to him ; he was so charmed
with her, that he would run a mile any time to
look at her bonny face ; his affections were entirely
won by her,—which was, by the way, no little
pleasure to herself, inasmuch as she regarded him
with very similar feelings.

There seemed quite a propriety in the mutual
affection of these two young people ; it was, to say
the least of it, quite patriarchal that Abraham
should love Sarah ; but whether Abe ever thought
of Scripture precedent for indulging such sentiment
or not, one thing is certain, he followed the example set by one of old, and took Sarah to be his
wife.

The wedding took place on the 10th May, 1818.
There was no extravagant or improvident display on the occasion. Abe did, however, put on
his best clothes, and stay from work for that day ;
and Sally, as he now began to call her, appeared
in a stuff dress, that served as her Sunday frock for
a long time afterwards. A few friends attended
the ceremony by invitation, and a few more of the
gentler sex just dropped in as they were, to see
that the affair was properly done, as well as to
indulge a pardonable liking for that kind of

religious service. Some of them probably never attended a place of worship except on such interesting occasions, or in connection with a christening. Here, then, was an opportunity for these people to indulge their select tastes, and they failed not to embrace it.

The ceremony over, the happy pair came forth to be pelted, according to custom, with rice and old shoes, symbolizing the wishes of the bystanders, that all through life they might enjoy plenty, prosperity, and good luck. Then came the walk home through the village arm-in-arm ; Abe nervous, and Sally blushing under the kind yet familiar congratulations of their friends.

The day was spent in a quiet, happy manner among the members of the wedding party, and nothing particular occurred until a little before seven o'clock in the evening, when all at once Abe got up, reached down his hat, and prepared for going out.

" Where's ta going ? " someone asked. Sally was looking at him rather curiously, as if she could not understand his movements.

" Why," said he, " doant yoa know it's my class noight ? "

" Well, what by that ? they'll niver expect thee t'-noight."

" Oh, but I mun goa."

All present laughed right heartily at his remark, and one of them said, " Nay, lad, thaa mu'nt goa

t'-noight and leave th' wife and all th' friends;
foak 'll laugh at thee."

"Let 'em laugh; th' devil 'll laugh if I doant goa,
and foak 'll laugh if I do. I'm sure to be laughed
at, ony way; I'll goa." He looked at Sally for a
moment, and saw, at any rate, that she understood
him, although she did smile; so opening the door
he shot out, saying, "I shalln't be long, lass." He
went to his meeting just the same as usual, and no
matter to Abe if his leader and class-mates were
all surprised to see him, he was quite as comfortable
as if a wedding were an every-day event with him.
Abe's maxim was to allow no hindrance to stand
in the way of his duty to God. Christ came first
with him, his wife stood next; and as he began, so
he continued through all his marriage life.

This worthy couple began housekeeping in a
very humble way,—it was really "love in a cot,"—
and with very limited means; but they were happy
in each other and happy in God. Sally made a
good wife, and contributed greatly not only to her
husband's happiness, but also to his usefulness in
the Church. Too much can hardly be said in
honour of that humble and devoted woman, whose
great study, during all their life together, was to
make home most attractive to her husband, and
his path, as a Christian, easy. When the charge
of a large family came upon them, she cheerfully
and studiously undertook the multitudinous little
offices and cares that always come, under the

circumstances, and threw as little as possible upon
her partner in the house; for she used to say,
" Dear man, he has enough to do to find us in
bread, without troubling to put it into our mouths."
Ah, and when there was scarcely even bread for
them, which often happened in those hard times,
she would scorn to murmur at her husband, or
utter a word that seemed like a reflection upon
him ; no, she was united to him " for better, for
worse," and she bore whatever came with a noble
and patient fortitude. Many a time, however, had
she, poor thing, to go to her heavenly Father with
her cares, and vent her anguish in a shower of
tears, which Abe never saw, and perhaps never
heard about; and when he came home from his
day's toil, she always tried to have a cheerful face
and a smile for the dear man.

Besides attending to the duties of her household
like an exemplary wife, she was often engaged in
her own house *burling* cloth for the manufacturers,
by which means she earned a scanty addition to
their income. Frequently when Abe retired to
rest, she would pretend she was scarcely ready,
and then, after he had fallen soundly asleep, she
might be seen by the dim light of a candle, hour
after hour, till far away into the morning, picking
at the cloth in order to get it finished; then, tired
in body and spirit, she would throw herself down
to sleep, and recruit for the struggles of another
day. Whenever the children had any new clothes,

which was too seldom, they were made by her
hands. Necessity had taught that thrifty little
woman many a thing, until in time she learnt not
only to earn and make their clothes, but even to
mend their shoes herself. Many a homely patch
did she put upon their clogs, and many a sole, too.
She had fingers for anything, and never stood fast
whatever came in her way. While many others in
her position would have sat wondering and de-
spairing, she arose, stuck to her task, got it done,
and if she had any time, she did the wondering
afterwards.

Go when you would to Sally Lockwood's house,
it was always tidy, and there was a clean chair for
you to sit upon. Although their clothes were coarse,
and patched with more pieces, if not more colours
than Joseph's coat, the children were always clean,
though many a time they hadn't a change of garment to put on. What that means in a large
family, the thrifty wives of hard-working men will
understand. The frequent late washings on Saturday nights, when the little ones were gone to bed,
were something wonderful, and what was even more
remarkable still was, that Sunday morning found
their things all clean and dried, ready for them to
go to school like other children.

Ah, Sunday morning, beginning of the day of
rest,—how welcome to poor Sally after her hard
week's toils and anxieties! When the family were
gone to school, and her honest man was some-

where at work in the Master's vineyard, she could
slip on her bonnet and shawl and just run into the
preaching service close by, and gather strength
and encouragement from the earnest prayers and
humble exhortations of those men whom God had
found in the quarry, at the loom, in the mine, or
at the lapstone, and sent forth Sunday by Sunday
into the villages to preach a homely gospel to the
poor, and comfort to His flock.

And thus she struggled on from week to week
and year to year, bearing with uncomplaining
fortitude her own burdens, and lightening, when she
could, those of her husband; setting an example
of patience, industry, and piety before her family,
thus by example, as well as precept, training them
up in the fear of the Lord.

No wonder that one of Abe's greatest boasts was
his wife. Next to his Lord and Master, whose
praise was ever on his lips, Sally came in for
honours. "Aar Sally," which was the usual homely
and affectionate way in which he spoke of her, was,
humanly speaking, his sheet anchor; her word was
more to him than counsel's opinion, and consider-
ably cheaper; what "aar Sally" said was Act of
Parliament in that little house. She had gained a
power there which was due to her, and which she
exercised for the benefit of the whole.

"Aar Sally" often figured in Abe's sermons, and
always in a favourable light, which shows the
estimation he cherished for the worthy partner of

his joys and sorrows. Although, as years went on,
time, labour, and anxiety made their unmistakable
impressions upon her, she was always bonny to
Abe; and up to the last, when he was a feeble
old man, and she was stricken in years, he used to
say, "Aar Sally is th' handsomest woman i' th'
world." It is possible that this assertion may have
been the occasion of some tender disputes in some
quarters, but nothing was ever heard to that effect,
and no one ever openly ventured to enter into
competition with Sally for the honour which was
ascribed to her, so that she was, *without dispute*,
the handsomest woman in the world.

> " Handsome is he, that handsome doth,
> And handsome, indeed, that's handsome enough."

Beauty is only skin deep, but goodness goes right
through. Sally was a good wife, a good mother,
a good Christian, and now her soul rests in the
presence of Him " who is fairest among ten thousand, and altogether lovely."

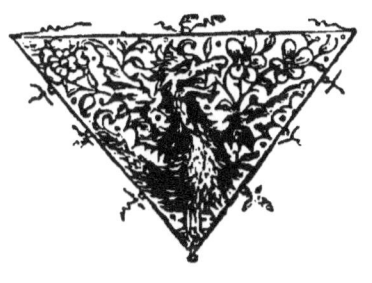

CHAPTER VII.

𝔚ind and 𝔗ide 𝔄gainst.

WHEN Sally gave her hand to Abe, we have said it was "for better, for worse," but she soon found there was a good deal of "worse" in it. What a sad thing it seems that nearly all the pretty castles which young people build for themselves in the air, should so soon fall to pieces! What a wonderful contribution it would be to the science of architecture if the ideas of these erections could only be realized in substance! Ah, but such is the nature of things, that castles without foundations can only be built in the air, and commonplace men are unable to do that. It has been a great disappointment to the constructors of these buildings, that they have never been permitted to spend a single hour in them; so very attractive as they looked, too, covered all over with gilt and flowers, and furnished in a style that outrivalled the pictures of the "Arabian Nights."

A real prince might be happy if he could only get
in. Some of them have taken years to bring to
such a state of perfection ; now, a little addition
is made here, and then a slight alteration there,
until it is finished, and the happy pair set off to
take possession of the fairy palace. But they never
enter it : the more eager they are to get in, the
more confused they become as to the position of
the doorway ; one thinks it is at the front, the
other fancies it must be at the side, and every time
they go around the house seeking the entrance, by
some mysterious means the house seems further
from them, and another effort is necessary to
reach it. How tiresome ! but they must be in, for
storms begin to gather, and they are not prepared
for them ; the wind blows and whistles as if calling
up other evil forces for mischief ; night, like a
dismal monster in a black cloak, and barefooted,
is coming on ; the pretty castle is fading out of
view among the darkening objects around,—quick !
quick ! we must be in, for the hour is wild. On
they hurry, and in their haste, they find an open
door and enter ; there is shelter and rest for them,
but when daylight comes they open their eyes,
and lo, the lovely castle is gone, and the home is
a weaver's cottage !

There is no doubt that Abe and his young wife
played their part at castle-building, like most
others in their position, and like others they found
it a great deal easier to erect than inhabit. How-

ever, there is this to be said for them, which cannot be said for all, they had fortitude to endure their lot without complaint; and though their castle was but a very little cot, it was commodious enough to hold them, and left room for a variety of joys and sorrows as well.

At the time when they were married, Abe was working as a cloth-finisher in a mill near Almondbury common, but not long afterwards, the work at this place failed, and he, with a number of others, was thrown out of employment. This was a sore reverse, for which they were ill-prepared. If trade had been good in the neighbourhood, he could easily have obtained work under some other master, but alas! the reasons which induced his employer to discharge his men, operated with others in the same way, and consequently left no opening for Abe.

What was to be done? Ah! that was the inquiry which often passed between Abe and Sally in their little home. The bread-winner was stopped, then the bread must soon stop, and then would come a dark *period*, that is, a full stop.

In their day of trouble they carried their case to the Lord, and asked His fatherly aid; many a time did they go together to vent their burden of trouble in His ear, and obtain strength to endure their trial. One day, after Abe had been in this way asking help and counsel of the Lord, he came and sat in a chair at one end of the table, while his wife sat near him, quietly stitching away at an old garment she was mending. For a few minutes neither of them spoke; by-and-by Sally looked up from her work to thread her needle, and their eyes met. She had a very sad look upon her face, for her heart was full of trouble, and she was just ready for what she called "a good cry;" but the moment she saw his face, which was covered all over with a comical smile, she caught the infection, and burst into a laugh,—a kind of hysterical laugh that had more sorrow than mirth in it. She laughed and he laughed, one at the other, till tears came from the eyes of both, and their poor sorrow-sick hearts seemed as if they would rise into their throats and choke them.

"Naa, lass, what's matter with the'?" at length exclaimed Abe.

"Why, it's thee made me laugh soa."

"Me, what did I do?"

"Ay, thaa may weel ask," said Sally, wiping her eyes with her apron. "Why, thaa looked a'most queer enough to mak' a besom-shank laugh; thaa's made my soides ache."

"Well, it 'll do thee gooid; thaa wants a bit of a change, for thaa's had heartache lang enough," responded her husband.

Sally resumed her work, but said nothing; her only response was a deep-drawn sigh. A few moments of silence again ensued, which Abe broke by saying, "Sally, haa would the' loike to see me wi' a black face?"

"What's 'ta say?"

"Haa w'd th' loike to see me wi' a black face?" repeated Abe.

"What art ta going to blacken thee face for doesn't th' like thee own colour? what does ta' mean?" inquired Sally looking at him.

"I mean," replied Abe with great earnestness, "that I'm gooin to turn collier."

"Nay, niver, lad!" cried his wife in dismay.

"Why, it's only for a bit till things brighten up in aar loine, and then thaa knows I can get wark at th' mill agean."

Poor Sally wept in earnest now; it was a shock to her feelings that she was not prepared for. At length she said, "I niver thought of thee goin daan a coil-pit, thaa isn't used to it, and thaa 'll happen break thee neck."

"Nay, not soa; I've warked mony a day in a coil-pit," said Abe. "Bless thee, my lass, when I were nowt but a bairn I used to wark i' th' pits; niver fear, I'm an owd hand, I can do a bit o' hewing wi' ony on um." And then when Abe saw the first burst of feeling on his wife's part was giving way, he went on to make good his position: "Thaa knows I mun do some'at, and there is nowt else I can see to turn to, and it 'll keep us going till I can get back to my own wark; we mu'nt be praad in these times, thaa knows. I'll promise to wesh th' black dust off my face every day," said he, laughing, and trying to get her to do the same. "Cheer up, my lass, we mun look th' rock i' th' face."

"Ah, th' Lord help us," responded Sally.

"Naa I like to year thee say that," said Abe, "because I believe it was the Lord that put it into my yead, for I niver thowt abaat such a thing till I were telling Him my troubles just naa, and then it came to me all in a moment, like as if some-one spake to me, and I says, I'll goa."

And he did go, and he got employment in one of the coal-pits in the neighbourhood, where he received so much per week as wages, and a lump of coal every day as large as he could carry home, as a perquisite. Of course he took as big a lump as he could manage, and sometimes he was tempted to overtax his strength. Many a time poor Abe had to stop on the way home, lift the coal down from his head, where he usually carried it, and rub the sore place; and many an expedient, in the way of padding, had he to resort to, in order to compensate for the soft place which nature, so prodigal in her gifts to some, had denied him. However, day after day he struggled along under his dark and heavy load, each day finding himself oppressed by another weight—of coals.

The new work was hard and trying to him, but he kept toiling on, and patiently waiting for the time when his heavenly Father would open up another sphere for him; meanwhile there was this consolation, that his toils kept fire in the hearth, and bread in the cupboard at home, and knowing this he was happy. He didn't envy any man his wealth, or his ease; he many a time on his way home, with the lump of coal on his head, was happier than the rich employer who passed him in his carriage; he had no ambitious schemes with which to harass his mind, his highest object was to glorify God in a consistent Christian life, and try to lead others to do the same. When his day's work was ended, he could lift his burden on his head, and journey homeward with a light heart; the only weight he felt was upon his head; many a day he came over the ground singing, certainly *under a difficulty*, but no matter, he did sing. Abe was an alto singer in the chapel choir, but in these homeward songs one would almost fancy he would have to take another part, as the lump on his head would render it rather inconvenient for him to reach the higher notes; ground-bass would be more in keeping with his circumstances, and probably he himself was more inclined to sink than soar; be that as it may, he sang and trudged along home, and any one that met him, might know he was happy as a king, aye, and happier than many.

CHAPTER VIII.

The Clouds begin to Break.

ABE had not long laboured in the coal-pit
before all about him began to feel he was a
good man. He did not hide his light from any one,
masters or men, and though they may not have
followed his godly example and Christian counsel,
they all respected him for his pious and consistent
life among them.

It so turned out that one day the foreman
ordered all the men to stay and work overtime at
night, in order to complete some important matter
which they had in hand. This was a terrible blow
to Abe, for it was his class-night, and he had never
yet missed that means of grace, nor would he,
if he could by any possibility get there; but now,
what was he to do? He felt it was his duty to obey
his master, and take his share of the extra work if
required; on the other hand, his heart yearned for
the fellowship of saints: how dear that little class-

room seemed to him then. All the day his mind dwelt upon the subject; he fancied his own accustomed seat empty, and his leader and classmates wondering why he was not there; he prayed earnestly for deliverance from this snare, and yet saw no way of escape. Evening came, and the usual hour for leaving work, but no bell rang the men out; on they all went at their task, and Abe along with the rest, yet all the time he was groaning in spirit; half an hour passed away, when the foreman came in. He was a hard, resolute man, that seemed to have neither fear of God nor devil before his eyes. "Abe Lockwood," said he, "isn't this thy class noight?" Abe looked up in an instant, and replied, "It is." "Drop thee wark this minute and go then; if I'm going to hell, I won't hinder another man from trying to get to a better place," and before Abe could find time to thank him, he was gone again. In a twinkling Abe was out of the place, and away over Almondbury common, like a fleet hound just slipt from the leash. He went to his class-meeting and was very happy there, but he did not forget in his own happiness to pray for the man who in this instance had bowed to the better spirit within him, and shown him such a mark of favour.

There is a heart in every man, however hard he may be, and when once the Spirit of God assails that heart, He may break it, or at least reason it into submission. We don't know all the power that God has, nor the many ways in which He can exert that power on the minds of men; we often hinder its operation by our want of faith. O Lord, increase our faith! Then "all things are possible to him that believeth."

For some time Abe continued working at the coal-pit. Although he made no complaints, he greatly disliked the employment, and looked forward with intense longing to the time when he could again return to his own calling. He told the Lord all his heart upon this subject, and often implored Him to lift him out of the pit and bring him again to the employment that was more congenial to his feelings. Nor did he pray in vain, as the following incident will show:—One day a gentleman came to the pit, and said, "Have you got a man here called Abe Lockwood?" On being answered in the affirmative, he expressed a wish to see him. Abe was at once communicated with, and fetched out of the place where he was working. On seeing him all begrimed with coal-dust, the gentleman said, "I'm sorry to see thee like this, Abe; I have been troubled about thee for some time."

"Have you, haa's that, maaster?"

"Why, I hardly know, but I have felt for many a day that I ought to come and offer thee work in my place, and now I've come, and if thou wants to leave here, I will find thee something to do in my mill."

Abe's grateful heart was almost in his throat; his eyes swam in tears, his face beamed with smiles, and he shouted, "Hallelujah! When mun I come?"

"Come at once if you can."

"All roight," said he, "I can leave here ony time. I'll come i' th' morning; bless th' Lord! I knew my Father would foind me another job somewhere."

That night he went home singing with the usual lump of coal on his head. When he got into the house he threw it down with a crash that startled Sally, his wife. "There," he said, playfully pretending to be vexed, "I'll fetch thee na moor coils on my yead, so thaa needn't expect it."

"What's matter wi' the' naa?" she said, looking at him.

"I tell the' I'll fetch the' na maar coils," he responded, rubbing his scalp as if it hurt him.

"Well then, we may as weel let t' fire goa aat first as last," rejoined the good wife, a little ruffled.

"Noa thaa shalln't. I loike a gooid foire as weel as onybody; and if thaa grumbles ony maar, I weant go to th' pit agean."

Sally looked hard at him for a moment or two, and in spite of the thick layer of coal-dust on his face, she could see there was a smile just underneath struggling to burst through. "What dost ta mean?" she said, half laughing herself.

"Mean!" exclaimed Abe, jumping from his

seat, and seizing hold of her hand, "Mean! Why, I mean that I've done with coil-pit; the Lord has gotten me a job in Huddersfield at my own wark, and I'm goin' in th' morning, bless th' Lord!"

Sally smiled, wiped her eyes, and said quietly, "Well I niver; aye, but I am glad; come and get thee teaa, my old collier." And that night there was sunshine in Abe's cottage hours after the great orb of day had gone down and left the world in darkness.

CHAPTER IX.

Salem Chapel.

CLOSE to the entrance of the village, at the top of the main street, and within five minutes' walk of the railway station, stands the Methodist New Connexion Chapel of Berry Brow. It is situated on the right-hand side of the street coming from Huddersfield; being on lower ground than the road, it has from this point a stunted appearance. Pursuing the decline and curve of the street a little further brings you to the vertex of a triangle of level ground, on the base of which the chapel stands. It is fronted by a graveyard, whose two sides gradually converge towards a little iron gateway at the entrance.

Seen from here the chapel presents a more pleasing appearance, though even now an observer could not fail to be struck with the dwarfish look of the building; there is a want of height to give it proper proportion. It shows a plain stone front, which suggests that the good people who built it had no money to spend in costly ornamentation. SALEM, the honoured name of the chapel, is inscribed on the front. The Sunday-school, which is of more recent date, stands adjoining it on the left; the foreground treasures up the dust of many pious pilgrims who, in the days gone by, came to this house of peace. The chapel has two doors in the front; inside, the appearance is exceedingly plain; the pulpit is stationed with its back against the front wall, and is enclosed by a pew that was formerly occupied by the choir, but now mostly by the speakers at the public meetings, for, being somewhat elevated, it serves as a permanent platform. The plan of the sittings is a simple rising gallery, springing from the floor half-way to the ceiling, and traversed by two aisles leading direct from either doorway; in a recess abutting through the right-hand wall, the organ is fixed. The chapel is capable of accommodating about three hundred persons, though there have been times when, somewhere or other, it has afforded room to much larger numbers of people that have crushed within its limited space. Altogether, it is a plain, unpretentious structure, by no means equal to the growing requirements of the prosperous Church that worships there in these days.

Salem Chapel, like many other places of worship, has its story, full of sacred incident and interest. It has been the religious birthplace of hundreds of

5

precious souls, many of whom are now in glory, while others are journeying thitherward. Many of the ablest ministers the Methodist New Connexion has ever had, have counted it a joy to preach in that old sanctuary.

Several revivals of the work of God have broken out within those walls, and spread with such rapidity and power through the neighbourhood, that Satan's strongholds have trembled before them ; and in the great day of the Lord it will be said of Salem, " This and that man were born . there."

But before it was built the people used to attend the High Street Chapel, Huddersfield, which involved a walk of over two miles each way, and this in unfavourable weather was no light task. The time came, however, when they began seriously to entertain the idea of having a place of worship in their own village.

Abe Lockwood was among the chief advocates of this scheme, and it was mainly owing to his activity in the matter that the undertaking was at length commenced and completed. In the month of July 1823, Abe, full of the new Chapel enterprize, entered a harvest field belonging to Mr. S—— of Armitage Fold, where several members of the Society were at work, and took upon himself to announce that there would be a meeting in a certain house that night, for the purpose of considering whether they were to have a Chapel in

Berry Brow. The meeting was held, and the decision taken in favour of the movement. They would arise and build, so in God's name they began the work.

It was a serious undertaking for them, as most of the members were poor working people, but they were in earnest, and at once opened a subscription list, each of them promising something to the fund before they went outside to solicit help from any one else. They then obtained further promises from others, and arranged to gather the money by weekly instalments, some being as little as a penny. Then, in order to save cost as much as possible, the men themselves went and delved in the quarry for stones, and borrowed horses and carts of the farmers to remove the material to the chapel site, and when it sometimes happened that they could not obtain the use of horses, they got the loan of carts, and the men, old and young, took the horse-work themselves, and drew the stones to the building place.

In all this Abe was a foremost worker, toiling early and late, and asking any one and every one to come to their help, by which means they got many of the wild young men of the village to assist in the work. This did not, however, meet with universal approval ; there were some few very good people, who mostly employed themselves in looking on, giving directions, and finding fault, who said it was not right to bring a lot of ungodly young men into a work so sacred ; they expostulated with Abe on the subject, he being the chief cause of their enlistment, but he replied, " Not roight for them to help in building th ' Lord's haase! It must be roight; if they soil th ' stones with their fingers, God will put them roight again when He gets into it. I wouldn't care if th ' devil hissen were to come and drag stones for th' place, if only Jesus is preached in it afterwards ; " so the croakers didn't gain anything by their complaints, except rejoinders from Abe, which taught them a little good sense, and they went on with the building.

The foundation stone was laid on Shrove Tuesday 1824, and the chapel was opened for religious services on Good Friday 1825. The Rev. Thomas Allin preached on that occasion with his usual extraordinary ability. From that time until now the cause has never looked back, but has maintained a steady onward course. Seasons of trial and depression have occasionally gathered over it like dark clouds, but the earnest band of Christian people it has drawn together, have been conducted under the clouds in safety, and have lived to come out again into the sunshine of prosperity.

There is not a trouble or a joy, not a throb of sorrow or a thrill of delight that ever came to that church during those years, which Abe Lockwood did not feel. He was so mixed and wrapt up in its history and workings that he counted its very pulsations as distinctly as he felt his own. In later

years, when other labourers were brought into the
church, and his services as a local preacher came
into greater demand, many of the duties involved
in conducting the cause fell into other hands ; but
Abe's love for Salem never did and never could
diminish ; to him it was the most beautiful sanctuary
in the Circuit or out of it ; and there it stands as
a monument of the zeal and devotion of those
earnest men who more than fifty years ago laid its
foundations, and reared its sacred walls in the name
of the Lord.

They are nearly all gone to their reward, Abe
among them, but in no sense more than this is the
Scripture fulfilled, " He being dead yet speaketh."

CHAPTER X.

Abe becomes a Local Preacher.

SEVERAL years had passed away from the
date of Abe's marriage, and a family of young
children had sprung up around him, filling his
cottage with life, and keeping him and his active
wife constantly employed to supply their daily
necessities. Hard times they had during those
years, but they held on their honest way, content
with what they got, and envying no one that was
in better circumstances than themselves.

During all these years Abe continued a devoted
follower of Christ; he was always at the means of
grace, and his chief aim was to be a true disciple
of the cross. At the same time he was slowly
acquiring ability to speak in the meetings with
more propriety and effect.

Methodist prayer-meetings and class-meetings
are excellent training schools for public speakers.
Most of the best ministers in Methodism first learnt

to talk in these little meetings, where they have had, week by week, opportunities of expressing their thoughts and feelings upon their religious life and experience ; and although there are some who have profited but very little by the benefits afforded in this way, there are many others who have made their way from that humble beginning up to the highest ranks of the Christian ministry.

In this training institution Abe slowly and steadily improved his powers, till some of his friends began to think he ought to have his name placed on the Circuit plan as an exhorter. It was accordingly mentioned to him, but for some time met with no very favourable response from Abe. "Come on t' plan," exclaimed he ; "nay, not soa, unless you want to mak' a clerk o' me ; but I can say Amen, without being planned."

However, circumstances sometimes happen which have more force of argument in them than any-thing that men can say. It occasionally transpired, that some local preacher who was planned to preach in Salem Chapel did not come to his appointment, and some person in the congregation had to take the vacant place, and conduct the service as well as he might be able without any previous prepara-tion. Now it appears that Abe found himself placed just in this very unenviable position. The congregation were all in the chapel ; the hour of service had come, and passed, yet no preacher arrived ; the people were whispering and looking at the clock; one brother went to the door to see if there were any sign of the preacher's coming; two or three of the leading brethren were whispering together, and then one of them came over to Abe and said, "I'm afraid there's going to be no preacher, thou'll be like to try and talk a bit this morning."

"Me, noa, I canna praach, mun," said Abe, evidently agitated.

"Aye, but thou can; thou'll have to try, and we'll pray for thee."

Abe turned pale, looked up at the little pulpit, then down on the ground, and then said, "I've now't to talk abaat, noa, I canna tak' it." Then another brother came and united his persuasion to that of the man already with him, and at length Abe arose and went into the singing pew in front of the pulpit, pale and trembling, and announced a hymn. The service began, and grew into a kind of compromise between a prayer meeting and preaching. The preacher took a text, and in his own style did his best to speak from the words,—the probability is he *did speak from them,* further from them than critical hearers would judge proper, but what of that? He did his best, and there were none in the congregation but knew him and knew his consistent life; and although what he said was very unpreaching-like, it did not matter; the people were well pleased, and Abe was very glad when it was over.

After the first time this occurred again and

again in Salem, until Abe began to be looked upon
as the general stop-gap, as they called him. But
he was not to occupy that post always; it was only
the stepping-stone to something else, for by-and-
bye some of the local preachers would take him
out with them to their appointments, and let him
talk to the people as well as he was able. Wherever
he went they said he must be sure and come again;
he was so quaint, droll, plain, yet withal so fervent,
that everyone enjoyed his remarks, and wished to
hear him again.

About the year 1833, and during the ministry
of the Revs. J. Curtis and G. Bradshaw in the
Huddersfield Circuit, an incident took place which
will give an idea of the style of Abe's early preaching efforts. It was on one Shrove Tuesday after-
noon that he had to preach at Paddock;—the service
was at that time conducted in a cottage;—a good
deal of talk had been indulged in by the people
in anticipation of Abe's visit, and a great amount
of curiosity and interest was excited. The place
was full. Abe arrived, rubbing his hands, and
blessing the Lord, and immediately took his place,
and commenced the service. His prayer was like
himself, rough and earnest; Divine power came
down upon the little company, and tears of joy
ran from all eyes. He selected a lesson with
which he was familiar, and managed the reading
very creditably. Abe then took his text, the subject being Abraham offering up his son Isaac on

Mount Moriah. Just at that moment the Rev. J. Curtis came into the service. Now the unexpected appearance of the Superintendent Minister, under circumstances like those, would have unnerved most young preachers, but it had no such effect on Abe; he no sooner set his eyes on him, than he said, "Naa thaa sees I'm at it, we're just baan off to Mount Moriah, and thaa mun goa too," and off he went in a style peculiarly his own.

He drew some very amusing pictures of the patriarch, his son, and the young men preparing for the journey; he had Abraham ordering the servant men to do this, fetch that, undo something else; he had a deal of trouble in saddling the asses, those animals exhibiting the obstinate tendencies for which their descendants are even yet so renowned; all was at length ready, Abraham and his attendants were mounted and setting off, when the door was again opened, and in walked the Rev. G. Bradshaw, the young minister. At sight of him Abe shouted, "Aye, lad, thaa art baan to be too late, we've gotten th' mules saddled and had a'most gone withaat thee, but niver moind, thaa mun catch a mule for theesen, and come on behind." So away they went, Abe taking the lead, and the people mentally following.

He preached them such a sermon as they had never heard in their lives—nor anybody else. Now they laughed at his odd sayings and grotesque pictures, and then with melting feelings they

praised God as they listened to some of the simple
yet truly beautiful sayings which fell from his lips.
As a sermon, there was enough to find fault with,
for he knew nothing about the art of sermonizing,
and cared as little ; but it was so full of homely
truth and spiritual feeling, that every one, ministers
not excepted, forgave the faults, and said it was a
means of grace.

In this way Abe continued for some time, occasionally preaching without being officially recog-
nized, but at length his name was placed on the
plan as a local preacher on trial. When the term
of his probation was almost expired, Abe was
required to preach one week-night in High Street
Chapel, Huddersfield,

HIS TRIAL SERMON.

It was a terrible trial for him, which appears
strange, considering how easy he felt when the
Circuit ministers heard him in the little room at
Paddock, yet so it was ; and as the time came
on, Abe thought he never could show his face in
High Street. Had it been anywhere else he would
not have cared, but he had a dread of the Circuit
Chapel. He had gone to several of the country
places during the year, and sometimes did very
well ; but then, he felt at home among the plain
village people ; they could understand his broad
vernacular, and make allowance for his blunders,
which he knew were not a few, but in High Street

everything was different. He thought they could not exercise the same forbearance towards him, and so he shrank from the task.

But then he remembered it was not a place of his own seeking; that it was a trial which other plain men had undergone before him, and would do again, and he could not expect more favour than his brethren; so he must go and do his best, trusting in the Lord for help. And that evening Sally brushed him up, and had his clogs polished, and away he went to Huddersfield. There was a good congregation to hear him, and among others several local preachers. Abe was very nervous, and everything around conspired to make him so. He was in High Street Chapel, awful; he had to preach, worse; to preach a trial sermon, worse than ever; before all these grand folks, and in the presence of the Superintendent, it was blinding, sickening, confounding. He started at the sound of his own voice, and when he tried to speak, he somehow said just what he didn't intend, and made more mistakes than he had either time or sense to rectify; then, whenever he moved his feet, his clogs clamped on the floor in such a way as he had never heard them anywhere else; he was in a fever of excitement and fear. However, he had to preach; so having announced his text, he commenced his sermon, but it was evidently hard for him to say anything; he tried and tried, rolled his eyes up and all around, clasped his hands, uttered a few sentences, scratched his head, and exclaimed, "Friends, I'm plogged" (meaning he could not go on), "she weant goa; if this is preaching trial sermon, I'll niver try another; we'll be like to swap texts" (try another text). Now while he was finding another text, the congregation sang a hymn, and by the time this was done, Abe was ready with his text, which he announced and again started to speak, but with no greater success, for it seemed as if all his ideas were gone wool-gathering. He coughed, stammered, and sweat at every pore, but brought forth nothing else; an encouraging word or two from one of the brethren was very welcome at that moment, for looking towards him, Abe said, "She weant goa, but we'll try another."

Twice breaking down in one service would have satisfied any ordinary man in his circumstances, and so daunted many as that they would never have been heard of again; but Abe was no ordinary man, and was not soon killed; he had come there to try to preach, and it was evident to every-one that he was trying; he knew that if he made another attempt he could not do worse than he had done, and he might do better, and if he did break down there would not be anything very unusual in it, seeing it would make the third time, so he found another text and announced it. Every-body was wide awake and ready for another stop, but Abe smiled, brightened up, and went on:

"She's baan to goa this time, I do believe," said
he, and so it proved, for when he got into his subject he spoke very fluently, sensibly, and naturally,
and all present felt that Abe could preach when
he got started, and how could he or any one else
preach without starting?

A short time after this eventful service Abe had
to pass through another trying ordeal. His case
had to come before the Circuit quarterly meeting,
the tribunal which has made many an innocent
man tremble. There he had to be examined as to
his acquaintance with and belief in the Methodist
doctrines, rules, etc. What may have been the
merits of this examination we are unable to state;
probably there was a good deal of leniency shown
by the meeting towards Abe. If he was deficient
on some points, he compensated in others; if he
could not define and defend all the articles of our
faith, he could believe them as fully as any one
else; be that as it may, there was no serious
objection taken to him on the ground of his examination, but the affair of the trial sermon was not
so soon got over, and a good deal of special plead-
ing had to be done for him by his friends, which is
no unusual thing when the merits of a candidate
are under discussion. That "swapping of texts"
no less than three times was a very extraordinary
feature in the case, and called forth some severe
censures. A man that did so could not be fit to
come on the Circuit plan as an accredited local

had prayed earnestly, and had retired from his rural sanctuary, the hidden and moveable part of his congregation were glad to get away. Some of the callous ones endeavoured afterwards to chaff Abe about the open-air service, but most of them were glad to say nothing on the subject, inwardly determining never again to venture profanely within the sacred precincts of the good man's sanctuary.

Abe gradually grew in the esteem of the people throughout the entire Circuit, so that his coming to preach was quite an event of interest among them. They knew he was in earnest for his Master's glory; and though he sometimes said and did things which some men would shrink from, and some would condemn if done by others, no one was displeased at them in little Abe. He was a favourite, and special privileges were accorded him, so that he could say and do just as he pleased. He knew this quite well, and, though he seldom fell into the error of using it as a license, it had the effect of bringing him out in his own true character.

Sometimes he became very happy in the pulpit, and fairly jumped for joy. He was preaching at Shepley, and, as was his frequent custom, he had a brother local preacher in the pulpit with him, to assist in the preliminary exercises. On this occasion our old friend T. Holden acted as his curate. Abe was blessed with great liberty during the delivery of the sermon : he wept, clapped his hands, stamped his feet, and rattled his clogs together.

Brother Holden shuffled about to make room for
him as well as he could in the narrow area of the
pulpit, but he was not quick enough ; down came
Abe's foot on the curate's toes, almost capsizing
the preacher, without in the least disconcerting him.
"Moind thee toas, lad, steam's up, I mun jump
a bit." And he did jump, the more freely, too,
when his assistant retired from his exalted position,
and left him all the pulpit to himself. It is evident
from this little event just narrated, and others which
might be given, that Abe did, in time, overcome
his nervousness in the pulpit; being "plogged," and
"breaking down," became things of the past, and
he began to feel as much at home in the pulpit as
in his own house. So far did he show that " practice makes perfect."

CHAPTER XII.

" Butterfly Preachers."

A BE had no sympathy with men who allowed
themselves to be called preachers, and yet
could treat with indifference the work which was
allotted to them on the Circuit plan ; men who
seldom made their minds up to go to their work,
until they saw what kind of weather it was likely
to be ; men who didn't like going out in the rain
for fear of getting damp, nor in the wind because it
exhausted them, nor in the sun because it broiled
them, nor in the dark for fear they might miss
their way. He called them " Butterfly preachers,"
and often declared he would be ashamed to be
counted among them.

Yet he did not lay all the blame of their conduct upon the shoulders of these men, because he
thought the people helped in some measure to put
" butterfly notions " into their minds. If a good
man came to his appointment through the rain

and wind, and got somewhat badly used by the
weather, someone was almost sure to say something to frighten and dishearten him from ever
doing so again. "Oh dear, have you come in all
this rain? Well, I hardly thought you would be
here; nobody could blame you for staying at
home on such a day; you are very wet, you'll be
sure to take cold and be laid up," and Abe used
to say that kind of talk was enough to give a chill
to any man, and tempt him to stay at home next
time for fear it might rain.

It did not make any difference to him, however;
he went in all weathers, rain or sunshine, winter
and summer. There is a little ditty he used to
sing—

> "Come rain or come blow,
> A Methodist preacher, I must go."

One Sunday morning he was planned to preach at
Shepley, and it was pouring down rain. He, however, set off under his umbrella; but long before
he reached his destination he was drenched to the
skin. Prior to going into the chapel he called at
the house where he was going to dine that day;
the good woman was grieved to see him in such a
condition. "Dear me," said she, "you are almost
drowned; come in, take your wet clothes off, and go
to bed." "Nay, nay," replied Abe, "yo' mun't tak'
me for a butterfly preacher; I'm noan going to bed
i' dayloight, I'm baan to praach." And turning to

her husband, who was a big man, he said, " Thaa
mun lend me some o' thy claathes." The proposal
to adorn himself in his host's clothes seemed so
ridiculous, considering that Abe was a little man,
that both husband and wife laughed right out.
" Aye," said the man, "thou would look a queer
butterfly going into th' pulpit in my wings." But
Abe wasn't to be put off: "Come," said he, "thaa
mun foind me some o' thy claathes." They found
him a spare suit, and in a few minutes he came
downstairs fully attired, and presenting such a
figure that the man and his wife were almost ill
with laughing at him. It signified nothing to
Abe who laughed or who didn't; off he went to
chapel. He was a few minutes late, and most of
the congregation were in their places. He was
therefore very eager to get to the pulpit; but in
going across the chapel for this purpose, one of his
borrowed shoes slipped off, which brought him to
a sudden standstill, and caused special attention to
be drawn to his singular outfit; and the moment
the people comprehended the state of things, it
was impossible to suppress a laugh in old or
young; and yet while they laughed at his odd
figure, their hearts warmed towards him as they
thought of his zeal in coming so far, on such a
day, to preach to them.

That morning Abe had a good time in the
pulpit. He was very lively, and knocked about a
good deal; but it was noticed that he had frequently

to be looking down on the pulpit floor, and shuffling about with his feet. It afterwards came ·ut, that, in his excited moments, he had dropped his shoes off, and in getting them on again, had mixed them, and put his feet into the wrong receptacl s This occasioned him a considerable amount ʼf inconvenience, which ultimately exhausted his patience. He kicked the shoes aside, and said, " I have been trying all th' mornin' to stand in another man's shoes, and I canna' manage it; I'm in borrowed claathes, too, but, thank God, my sermon is my own." This little diversion set him off in another direction, and he turned the incident to such good and practical account, showing that Jesus once stood in our place and bore our stripes, that many have long remembered that service with very great pleasure.

TOILING ON.

On one occasion, when going to a distant appointment, his zeal was put to the test in such a degree that surely he would have been excusable if he had turned back and gone home again. Abe had a dread of disappointing a congregation. He used to say, "If I slip them once, two to one they'll pay me back; noa, I mun goa."

He had to set out one Sunday morning in a pelting rain for a walk of about six miles. It had been raining more or less for several days; the roads were in a sad condition for a " travelling praacher," as he often styled himself. The streams by the roadside were swollen over, and pouring their abundance out on the highroad, until it was very little better than a bog. Under these circumstances the wet soon found its way through Abe's boots and clothes. "Ne'er moind," he said to himself, "I'll find some dry claathes when I get there." So on he went over the rough bleak hill that wouldn't afford shelter for a rabbit, much less for a man, down the steep slope, through the running gutters of water. "Aye dear," said he, "I'm weshing my feet withaat taking my booits off." At the bottom of the hill, known as Stone's Wood Bottom, he was brought to a standstill. Along this bottom runs the river which takes the course of the valley through Berry Brow, before named; it was here spanned by a good strong bridge, having a wall on either side. The water in the river had risen so high with the rainfall, that it ran right over the bridge at both ends, and threatened to carry it away; all the low ground about the bridge was under water to some depth, and hereby Abe was brought to a halt. His only way was over that bridge, and now that was not available. "Well," thought he, "I'm done this time; haa can I get over?" Further up and down the river was swollen over its boundaries, and was out into the fields, while at the bridge it rushed along like a torrent. "Naa, Lord," Abe began, "Thaa knows where I'm plann'd to-day, and Thaa knows this is my only rooad to th' place; that's Thy watter, and I'm Thy sarvant; I mun be over somehaa; tak' care o' my body while I try." And into the water he plunged, and made straight for the bridge. On reaching this he tucked his umbrella under one arm, and climbed up on the wall of the bridge, and scrambled across on his hands and knees, while the torrent rushed along underneath at a horse-pace. Had he fallen into the water he would probably have been found drowned on one of the banks down the river, but it was not permitted. " Bless the Lord," he exclaimed, when he was safe on the other side, " I'm over! Ah! but I'll do better nor that when I come to pass the swellings o' Jordan! Hallelujah! I'll go over Jordan withaat wetting a threead on me!"

So thou wilt, Abe. Jordan's waves could not harm a brave, God-fearing, and God-honouring man like thee; they know a true-born saint by the tramp of his foot in the darkest night of death, and on his approach, they fall back into line like Royal Guards when the king goes past.

> " Though waves and storms go o'er my head,
>   Though strength, and health, and friends be gone;
>   Though joys be withered all and dead,
>   Though every comfort be withdrawn;
>   On this my steadfast soul relies,
>   Father, Thy mercy never dies

CHAPTER XIII.

Various Ways out of Difficulties.

ALMOST any one can get into trouble, but it
is not always so easy for any one to get out
again. Abe knew both ways,—the way in and the
way out,—and many a time he had to run the
gauntlet, and save himself as best he could.

There is an amusing story told of a little pas-
sage which the Rev. P. J. Wright once had with
him. They met on a Sunday morning at the
Honley railway station. Mr. Wright was at
that time Superintendent of the Circuit, and was
on his way to preach at Woodroyd, whilst Abe
was going to Honley on a similar errand. After
exchanging the ordinary salutations, the reverend
gentleman said, "Well, Abe, what are you going
to give them at Honley this morning?" On being
informed of Abe's subject, he further inquired how
he intended to treat it; whereupon his companion

began to give an outline of his sermon. When he had finished, his interrogator rejoined, "Why, you are wrong, altogether, Abe, you must change the order of your divisions, and put the first last, and the last first; you have got the cart before the horse." "Ne'er moind," said Abe, "I'll back her up th' hill. Good-morning, sir." "Cart before the horse" was no insuperable difficulty with Abe; he knew how to manage his own pony, and must drive in his own way; he was not very particular which came first so long as he could "mak' her goa." He took what suited his mind best, and paid very little attention to the rules of sermonizing; he was in this respect a law unto himself, and the favour with which his humble ministrations were received was a sufficient excuse for him.

We have heard a sermon described as a thing having three or more heads; it is said to be sometimes altogether void of body or matter of any sort; at other times it appears as a skeleton, without form or comeliness, having only the barest outline. Perhaps this in some measure explains why some people so seldom attend our places of worship; they fear to come *within the reach* of a sermon, and therefore stay away,—they have heard of some persons that have been *actually struck* with a sermon, and of others *being fastened to their seats* by it; how dreadful! Ah, anything will do for an excuse when people don't want to go to the Lord's house: "a poor excuse is said to be

better than none at all," but in this case we doubt
the wisdom of that saying.

Abe Lockwood was not very particular about
the number of heads in his sermons, or whether
they had any heads at all; his care was that
the sermon should have some soul in it, where-
from mainly resulted his power in the pulpit.

There is sometimes very great danger of sermonizing all the force out of a discourse; making
it so very proper that it serves more as an orna-
ment than a thing of practical use; it appears
more a work of *art* than a work of *heart*. Abe
didn't profess to understand the rules of sermonizing, nor did he make any particular effort in that
direction; as may be supposed, therefore, he was
often disconnected and irregular, but he knew
nothing about it, and nobody else cared; people
liked him as he was. His sentences were not like
beautiful stones turned and polished by the hand
of a lapidary, but they were rough lumps, in all
shapes, broken from the great rock of Gospel
truth, having their sharp points and jagged edges
on them; the consequence being that when slung
from the hand of this humble champion they left
a mark wherever they struck. He didn't care for
that round, smooth kind of preaching which always
rolls off; he liked the word to strike, mark, and
abide where it fell. He had no sympathy with
high-flown sermons which shut out the Cross of
Jesus and those good old Gospel truths associated

with that dear emblem of God's love to the world. If such a discourse were delivered in his hearing he was sure to say something about it. " Praacher brought us a lot of butterflies and fancy birds and let 'em fly abaat th' chapel, and while we wore starin' abaat after th' birds, we niver gat a soight o' th' Cross."

A young student from Ranmoor College came to preach at Berry Brow. Abe was in the vestry waiting to see him before he went into the pulpit. He shook him warmly by the hand and blessed him, then added in his own droll but kind way, " Naa, my lad, don't let's hav' ony starry heavens t' day, tak' us t' th' Cross !" Had Abe known this young man he would also have known there was no need to exhort him to " tak' them t' th' Cross." The fact was, Abe didn't want to follow any astronomical preacher all through the heavens, striding from star to star with scales in his hand trying their weight, sizes, and distances! " The Cross " was his watchword and rallying-point; there he loved to begin, and there he would always end. Christ the Redeemer was his star, and in the clear unclouded view of that Divine orb he was happy whoever was the preacher.

"PUCKER IT IN, LADS."

In his pulpit exercises Abe generally enjoyed great self-command, and things which would have disabled many a man in the same position, had little or no effect on him. This was not always the case, as we shall have occasion to show, but usually nothing disturbed the even balance of his mind. We have already seen how if a text "wouldn't goa," he could "swap" for another that would "goa." So if he failed to get hold of a thought which had been in his mind before, he did not trouble himself about the matter; he would just tell the people "he had forgotten th' next idea," and then pass on to something else.

His self-possession stood him in good stead one day, and helped to carry others through a trouble as well. He was in one of the country pulpits, and had just announced the second hymn, which was a long metre. The choir commenced to sing a common metre tune to the hymn, but before they had got through the second line they found out the mistake, and one after another dropped their voices and ceased to sing. One tenacious brother, who did not like to be beaten, held on, and made a jumble of the words for a few moments, and then he stopped; whereupon Abe clapped his hands, and turning around to the choir, he exclaimed, " Ne'er moind, lads, pucker it in ! pucker it in ! Onybody can mak' a long metre tune goa to a long metre hymn, but yo' mun beat that," and then he joined heartily in the puckering exercise, and helped them through their trouble.

"BREAD OF LIFE FREE."

At another time he had been preaching about
the Gospel being the bread of life for the world,
and showing up its qualities and worth; especially
did he dwell upon its freeness for all, that it could
be had "without money and without price;" this
was his last point, and he made much of it. Now
it so happened that immediately on concluding his
sermon he had to announce a collection. On
sitting down in the pulpit while it was being made,
the thought flashed into his mind that he had con-
tradicted his own teachings by announcing that
collection. He knew where the snare had come
from, and at once in his own way broke it asunder.
Rising again to his feet and bending over the pulpit
front, he cast his eyes around the chapel as if
trying to find someone. "I know that voice," he
began, "it's the devil's." Every eye was on him in
a moment. "What does thaa say?" "That I ha'
not been spaking th' truth, because I telled them
th' bread of life wor free, and naa I'm asking th'
people to pay for it. Thaa knaws as weall as I do
th' bread is FREE, but we mun pay for th' baking.
Mak' th' collection, friends, to pay for th' baking,
and ne'er moind him." We need hardly say the
people gave willingly to this collection, for they
knew very well that though the Gospel was free to
the whole world, expenses were incurred in carrying

on God's work which they should help to disburse, so Abe got out of that difficulty.

"MY GOD SHALL SUPPLY ALL YOUR NEED."

The Wesleyan Superintendent Minister was planned to preach one week-night near Berry Brow, and on some account he could not attend. A substitute had to be found, and Abe was waited on during the day, to see if he would act in that capacity. "I'll try," he said, and accordingly when the time came he set out for the chapel. Some of the congregation knew who was to preach, others did not. At length the door opened, and in walked Abe, and made straight for the pulpit, clamp, clamp, with his wooden clogs on the floor and up the pulpit stairs. He began the service with the usual smile on his face; then he announced his text, "My God shall supply all your need," and closed the Bible as he always did as soon as the text was read. "Naa," said he, "I knaw some o' yo are disappointed at seeing me here instead of your praacher, but it was oather me cr nobody. Naa, if th' travelling praacher had come to-noight, he moight easily ha' praached a much better sermon than I can, but I'll defy him or onybody else to foind a grander text than this; it's a raight un, and it's your own fault if you doan't get some good aat on't : if the Lord had thought you *needed* it, He would have sent you somebody better than me, for He will supply all your need." The con-

7

gregation saw at once the condition they would
have been in if Abe had not come to their help.
They smiled at his remarks, and from that moment
forgot their disappointment, nor did they think of
it again during all that service. Thus Abe's tact
in managing people helped him happily through
this difficulty, as it had through many others in his
lifetime.

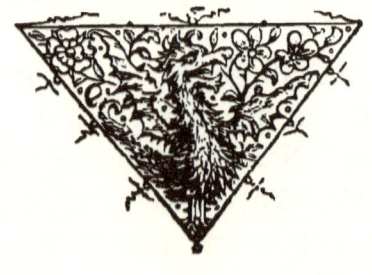

CHAPTER XIV.

Abe's Titles and Troubles.

IT is time we said something on this subject, as we are come to the stage in his life when he began to be known by various dignified ecclesiastical titles. He loved his own plain name, Abe Lockwood, better than any other, and therefore wanted no improvement. That was the name in the roll of the Church, and that was the name written in the Lamb's book of life; he wanted no other. If any one addressed him as Mr. Lockwood he would often break in, "They call me Abe Lockwood!" and this was no pretended humility on his part, but the expression of a sincere preference for the name by which he had always been known among his friends : but the time came when it was impossible for him to resist the universal custom of saluting him by some title, so he had to yield to the inevitable.

A story is told, how that on one occasion a

parcel of clothes came to the house for his wife and children. It was wrapped in strong brown paper, and on the address-label was written, "Abraham Lockwood, Esq." Soon after this, he was taking part in a public meeting in the place from which the present was supposed to have come, and in his speech he thanked the unknown donor; and having done this, he proceeded to correct a mistake which, he said, had occurred; the person who sent him that parcel had addressed him as Esquire. "Naa," said he, "I doan't stand much upon titles, but if I am to have ony, I think I ought to have what falls to me by my birth. Yo' know, I'm a Prince of th' Royal Family, I'm a King's Son, my Father is th' King of Glory, and no man can say that, unless he is born of God, and I am, Hallelujah!" Although there may not be anything original in this, yet the happy way in which he worked it into his speech, and the use he made of it to show the necessity of the new birth, was exceedingly pleasing.

The title of "Bishop," or "Bishop of Berry Brow," was one of those by which he became familiarly known. This arose out of the position he held in the society there, almost like that of father among the members, and also from the amount of preaching he did all over the Circuit. Although this very reverend title brought him no increase to his stipend, nor any change in his social standing, it helped to show the general feeling with which he was everywhere regarded.

But the designation by which he was most familiarly known was " LITTLE ABE." This came into every-day use, and was unconsciously adopted by almost every person either in speaking to him, or speaking of him. Even the little children in the streets and in the Sunday Schools, hearing it from their elders, insensibly fell into the habit of styling him " Little Abe."

As this title is somewhat expressive of size, it may be well to convey some idea of

ABE'S PERSONAL APPEARANCE

He was below the average height and of slender build, yet withal a tough little man, and capable of performing as much work, and enduring as great fatigue, as men who are much bigger and stouter made. Abe used playfully to say, "Good stuff is mostly wrapped in small parcels." "A penny is a great deal bigger than a sovereign, but yo' all know which to tak' when yo' have your choice." "I'm nobbut a little un, but bless God, I'm big enough for th' Holy Ghost to dwell in." "I doan't tak' up much room in th' world, but I'm as happy as if I were as big as Berry Braa Church." "I'm a little un mysen, but my Father is greater than all."

His face was one of the happiest it was ever our good fortune to meet with. A smooth, round, ruddy, comfortable face, over which the razor had almost unlimited sway; his mouth was always in shape for a smile; his eyes were of a light blue colour, and twinkled with life and vivacity; his hair was always brushed back behind his ears, terminating behind in a pretty little natural curl, and whether it had the black gloss of his younger days, or the snowy white of old age, it was always neat and orderly. In early life he was very proud of his hair, and bestowed a great deal of care in its cultivation and arrangement. When he became converted, Abe's hair underwent a marvellous change. The beautiful locks which had been so much admired and preserved with such care, were roughly taken off by the family scissors and thrown into the fire, and while they frizzled into smoke, Abe felt he had done the right thing in casting down every idol and putting away every mark of pride. Many and many a time in after years would he say to his wife, "Naa then, lass, where's th' shears? Thaa mun clip my locks agean. Samson gat clipt by his wife, and he were worth nought after, but thy shears mak's me strong." Then Sally would gently snip the ends of the curling fringe all around, while Abe, by way of encouraging her, would put in, "We mun shun th' appearance of evil, thaa knows; cut a bit more, lass;" and then she would very reluctantly sever another lock or two, until he could be persuaded enough was taken off.

Abe was in the latter part of his life particularly neat in his attire, wearing an orthodox suit of black cloth, and cut in the Methodist preacher style. He wasn't at all sparing in white neckcloth, for he wore one that travelled around and around his neck in such profusion, that it might have been intended as an extra security against the loss of his head. Altogether he was quite the type of an old-fashioned Methodist preacher. In the pulpit his appearance was exceedingly prepossessing; he always had a smile on his face while talking, as if he thoroughly enjoyed the good news he was telling to others. In beginning to speak, or when about to say something which he thought particularly good, he had a way of holding his head a little over on one side, and clapping his hands together. These movements, accompanied with an occasional shrug of his shoulders, were among the general signs that the " Little Bishop " was having a good time, and when Abe was happy in his work, every-one that heard him had a liberal share of enjoyment and profit as well. But of course, like other men, he sometimes felt the misery of preaching in what he quaintly and appropriately called

"THE TIGHT JACKET."

Taking into account the want of education from which he suffered, the disadvantages he was at in preparing for his public duties, as well as other occasional depressing circumstances, we cannot wonder that he should sometimes have been the subject of the most painful restraints, likened by him to a "tight jacket." There was a wonderful difference in his preaching when he had one of these "hard times," and when he enjoyed liberty. If in the latter mood, as was generally the case, his tongue was like the pen of a ready writer, and streams of beautiful truth, sparkling with pious humour and accompanied with striking original illustrations, would pour from his lips; but if he had the "tight jacket" on, he could scarcely say anything, and it was a pain to listen to him.

Poor Abe had one of these "pulpit fevers" in Salem Chapel one day, and Sally, his wife, was there; she sat all the time in a nervous torment, and as soon as he had finished, she rushed off out of the place ashamed of him. Dear woman, her homely criticisms were sometimes very severe upon him, partly because she was jealous for his reputation, and partly because she so loved him, and that was her way of showing the ardour of her affection; she used a liberty which by some universal law falls to the right of all affectionate wives whose husbands are preachers, and she occasionally said some very terrible things to him about his sermons. On this particular day, therefore, Abe knew pretty well that when he got home he would get something besides his dinner. He winced as he thought about it, and made the walk home as long as he could, in the hope that *some-*

thing might cool down a bit ; however, he had to
go in, so, shrinking into the smallest possible
dimensions, he glided silently into the house, hung
up his hat, and sat down. Sally was in a flutter,
she was full, it must come :—" What hast ta been
trying to do this mornin' ? " she began, looking hard
at him.

"Why, I couldn't mak' her goa a bit somehaa,"
meekly replied her good man.

"Goa! No, haa does th' think she could goa,
thaa niver gat her on her feet."

Abe made no response, but sat mute in his
misery, and poor Sally felt a reaction setting in,
which made her feel as if she had allowed her
ardent affection for him to carry her too far.
Meanwhile, she was bustling about preparing the
dinner, and when all was ready, she went over to
him, and kissed his forehead, adding, "Naa, lad,
come and get th' dinner, and don't moind what
folk say ; thaa'll do better next toime, th' Lord help
the'." Abe was healed by a touch.

Ah, but he didn't like those dry, hard times,
when he couldn't find a handful of green-meat to
give to the Lord's dear sheep, and it would trouble
him deeply to think that he had led the flock to
expect green pasture, whereas he had only brought
them to feed among rocks and stones. Then the
old enemy would beset him, and say what an old
fool he was to think he could preach; that the
people only laughed at him and made sport of his

sayings, and that he had better give up preaching, and try no more. But Abe would say, "Why, devil, thaa 'rt vary much troubled abaat my praaching; if I'm such an old fool as thaa mak's aat, I canna do the' so much harm." But all the banter and strife he had with the devil did not conquer that arch-enemy; talking to him is mostly waste time and ill-spent breath; there is another way which a good man has of finding relief; he can go to God in prayer. This was Abe's sure refuge; here he vented his trouble, here he got comfort, here he gained fresh strength, and when he came warm from the closet struggle to the pulpit work he was another man. After passing through one of these temptations, he was almost sure to tell the people, the next time he preached, how the devil had harassed him, and wanted him to give up preaching, but how the Lord had bidden him to go on, and on he would go and did; his restraints were broken, his tongue loosed, and his soul fired, it was a joy to hear him then.

He was one day rejoicing in his regained liberty, when he said, "Aye, bless yo', I wor as fast as a thief in a man-trap; I couldn't get away till th' Lord came and let me aat." And then turning upon the unsaved part of his congregation, he used a simile, which, on his behalf, I claim to be original if not elegant. Said he, "Yo' may think I was fast enough, but let me tell yo', not hoalf as fast as some of yo' sinners. Yo' are like a flee" (fly) "in a

treacle-pot; the more he kicks the faster he sticks."
And there was truth in the saying, and although
the figure might amuse, the moral would remain
in many a mind for after-thought.

THE BLACK CLOTH SUIT.

When Abe had been some time preaching, and
was making a good name for himself in the Circuit,
a desire began to be felt by many of the friends
to hear him in High Street Chapel, Huddersfield.
This was before the present splendid sanctuary was
erected. Accordingly when the next plan came
out, he was appointed to take a Sunday morning
service. Many a time did he tell of the conster-
nation both he and Sally felt on making this
discovery. He was sitting at the end of the table
one evening with the plan in his hand marking off
his work, and his wife was busy about something
in the room, when, all at once, Abe exclaimed,
"Eh, lass, what dost ta think they've done?"

Sally looked rather startled and said, "Who?
what?"

"Why, they've plann'd me in High Street on
a Sunday mornin'."

"Niver!" gasped Sally, coming to look at the
plan herself; "where is it?"

He placed his finger on the number which indicated his work, and she saw it was a fact.

"Well," she said, "thaa canna goa; thaa has no
claathes fit to wear amang them grand foak."

Now Abe would never have given his clothes a thought if she had not brought the matter before his mind in the way she did; now, however, he remembered his coloured suit and his thick boots, and felt they were scarcely befitting the place he was called to occupy, however well they might do among plain people in the country places. At length he said, "But if I'm plann'd, I mun goa, and if they don't loike my claathes, I canna help 't." Meanwhile the date of the High Street event drew near, and the following Sunday would find "Little Abe" at his post of duty. He was far more anxious about his work than his appearance, so that all the care on this matter fell upon his wife. She was bothered sadly about his clothes. Saturday came, and, poor thing, she was bestowing especial attention upon his old coat, mending button-holes, cleaning spots out, brushing, shaking, and scrutinizing the old garments as she had never done before. That evening they were sitting together, just before Abe went out to the Band Meeting in the Chapel; a loud knock came to the door. In a moment Sally opened it, and a man handed her a large parcel, simply saying, "That's for Mr. Lockwood," and immediately went away.

"What's this?" exclaimed Sally, feeling and patting the parcel.

"Nay, lass, don't ask me; thaa mun open 't, and then I'll tell the'."

A table-knife soon severed the string by which

it was tied, and the good woman proceeded with
nervous fingers to unfold the wrapping, and out
came a black cloth suit for her husband. Neither
of them could speak for a moment or two ; she
lifted her apron to wipe her eyes; Abe's lip
quivered, and his eyes brimmed over ; he couldn't
help it, big round tears fell on his clasped hands
as they rested on the table ; both of them looked
at the parcel. " Does the' see that ? " at length said
Sally ; "thaa'll look loike a travelling praacher naa,
lad."

That broke the spell. Up jumped Abe and
began to leap about the house, clapping, rubbing
his hands, and blessing the Lord. All the children
joined the chorus, laughing, jumping, and shouting
"Daddy's got some new claathes ! Daddy's got
some new claathes ! " and poor Sally, full of smiles,
holding up one garment after another, kept inter-
jecting, "Well I niver ! " " Law me ! " " Eh, dear ! "
Abe's heart was full, and he must needs empty it
before Him who had inclined some unknown
friend to send this handsome and appropriate
present just at the right time. From an inner
room the voice of the good man was heard going
up to God in grateful acknowledgment of His kindness; and the children were hushed into quietness
hushed,—hushed while Daddy was praying. The
next day Abe appeared in his new clerical attire,
and from that time was never without the requisite
black cloth suit in which to go about his beloved

Master's work. Oh, how much we may learn from a little incident like this—how much of humble trust in God under all the circumstances of life, how much assurance that "your heavenly Father knoweth ye have need of these things," and that "My God will supply all your need!"

CHAPTER XV.

A Basket of Fragments.

THE fame of "Little Abe" was not confined to his own Circuit, it spread among the villages and towns for many miles around, so that he was greatly sought after to preach anniversary and other sermons, and wherever he went the people felt he was "a man sent from God." There are some who well remember his first visit to Elland, and the delightful day they had with him in the Lord's house. His text was, "My God shall supply all your need." He read these words, and then clapped his hands together, while his face beamed with smiles. "Well," said he, "do you want me to praach ony after that? what can onybody say after Paul spakes? He says everything with once opening his maath; with one scratch of his wonderful pen, he writes more than I could spake in a lifetoime, if I were left to mysen, 'My God shall supply all your need.' Friends, there's nowt left, yo've gotton all in that, iverything yo' need, and I reckon you'r weel off."

From this simple and easy beginning, he gradually got away into his subject, explaining, illustrating, and applying his text in a way that warmed every heart. He was condemning the want of faith which characterized some professors : "Bless yo'," he said, "sooiner than aar God would see His faithful children want, He would mak' apple-dumplins grow on ash-trees." And then he exclaimed, "Don't yo' believe these words? Ah, 'tis nowt unless yo' believe; you might be eating th' dumplins and smackin' your lips on th' apples, but if you doan't believe, yo'll say it's a dream. Wake up, and believe naa, and you'll foind your maath is full of good things."

"DISH-CLOTH."

I have said that some of Abe's similes were not very elegant, and when the following is related, my readers will agree with me ; but they were well understood by the people among whom they were uttered. Speaking one day of the pardoning mercy of God, and showing that He does not grudgingly forgive the penitent sinner, Abe said, "Yo' womenfolk know haa to wesh a pie-dish, I reckon? Yo'll tak' th' dish and put it into th' hot watter, and then tak' dish-cloth and rub it raand and raand, insoide and aatsoide, till it's clean, and then yo'll wipe it wi' a clean towel, and mak' it look just loike a bron new dish ; and that's haa th' Lord does wi' a poor sinner : He gies him a plunge into th' Gospel fountain, weshes all his sins away, and brings him aat a bron new man." An old woman sitting there caught the figure in a moment, and responded energetically, "Maa th' Lord tak' th' dishcloth and wipe some aat here t'-noight ! " "Amen," exclaimed " the Bishop."

"TASTE AND TRY."

Abe's remarks on Psalm xxxiv. 8, " O taste and see that the Lord is good," etc., were very characteristic. " David was nooan a bad man to deal with ; he didn't try to deceive onybody and mak' them believe a lie, like th' devil does ; he says, yo' may 'taste and see.' Naa, that ought to satisfy yo' particular falk ; yo' loike to taste th' butter and cheese afore you buy, and if it's gooid, you say, ' I'll tak' a pund o' that ; ' naa, then, come and try if th' Lord is gooid. Aye, bless yo', He is gooid ! He's as fresh as th' morning dew, and sweet as new cream," and then with a quaint look he would add, " and there's a deal more on Him than you often foind on your milk."

He used to say that religion could be tested in two ways ;—you can taste it yoursen, and you can see it in others. See what it has done for your neighbours—how it has changed th' lion into a lamb, th' raving sot into a sober and happy man ; weshed th' tongue and purified th' heart o' th'

8

blasphemer, and filled th' maath of the dumb with
songs of thanksgiving, see!—"See that the Lord
is good!" Then raising his voice and reaching
out his arm he would exclaim, "There's noan so
bloind as those that weant see! but remember,
yo' weant always be able to play th' bloind man,
God will crack a thunderbolt close to your ear
some day, and yo'll open your eyes to see th'
judgment before yo', and then what will yo' say?"

His only aim in what he said was to reach the
people's hearts and bring them to decision for
Christ; that was the reward he coveted, nothing
more, nothing less; only let him see sinners coming
to Jesus, and he was happy. He would stay all
night by a penitent, and never leave until he knew
the poor soul was safe in the kingdom of God.
Time was nothing to him; the long, dark journey
home brought no misgivings to his mind. When
his work was done, and another soul safe in the
arms of Jesus, the humble village preacher would
take his stick, or, as he sometimes called it, his
pony, and set off home, where many a time he
arrived faint and tired in the dead of the night,
but with his soul full of that peace which only a
man feels who has ungrudgingly laid his last rem-
nant of energy at the feet of his Divine Master.

"Who's been Here?"

"Little Abe" used everything that came to hand
in order to make the Gospel plain, and enforce its

teachings upon his hearers. Zeal for the work, and a devout bias to his mind, enabled him to find religious teaching in many things, wherein perhaps others would never have discovered any.

He was in one of his sermons exhorting the people to watch against the devil, lest he should gain an entrance to their hearts and spoil the work of God. "Naa," said he, " I'll tell yo' some'at. Aar lads" (his own sons) "took a fancy for a bit of garden ; we had a little patch of graand by aar haase ; well, they set to wark, mended th' fence all raand, dug up th' soil, threw aat th' stones and rubbish, raked it over and marked it aat into beds, and planted flaars, and you may depend t' lads wor praad o' their wark ; for mony a week they kept doin a bit noights and mornin's to keep it raight. By-and-bye, flaars came into bloom, pinks, panseys, and other things came aat all over th' garden ; woren't they praad naa, and so wor I. One mornin', just afore we were going t' th' mill, th' big lad went aat to look at th' garden a minute, and th' first words he said wor, ' Who's been here ? Who's been here ? " Aat I went, and I wor raight grieved to see all th' garden spoilt, flaars broken off, little beds trampled aat o' shape, and th' wark of months all undone. I saw in a minute haa it wor : an owd ass had gotten in during th' noight and done all th' mischief. ' Haa could he get in,' said th' lad, ' th' fence was all roight and safe ? ' But I said, ' Did ta fasten th

gate last noight?' He looked at th' gate and said,
'I don't knaw, father.' Ah, that wor it, there wor
his foot-tracks through th' gateway. Ah, friends,
the devil is like an owd ass, goin' skulking and
shuffling abaat in th' dark when other folks are
in bed sleeping, and he is always trying to get
into th' Lord's garden and spoil th' flaars; yo'
may mend th' fence as much as yo loike, but if
you don't fasten th' gate, he'll be in and undo all
th' good wark in your hearts. Shut th' gate, and
fasten it; nail it up, raather than let th' owd cuddy
get in; he hates everything that is good in nature
and grace; he'll spoil th' best wark of God in a
single noight; th' track of his owd hoof means
mischief, and one of his kicks would lame onybody;
keep th' devil aat o' th' heart, fence it raand with
prayer; watch against th' enemy, and you'll be
roight noight and day."

"When a strong man armed keepeth his palace,
his goods are in peace" (Luke xi. 21).

"ELLOW! WHO'S THERE."

Abe had a very quaint and original way of
rendering the parable of our Lord on the importunate neighbour (Luke xi. 5).

"There was a good man who said one noight to
his wife, 'Naa, lass, we mun be getting to bed, I
ha' to be up i' th' mornin' i' good toime.' 'Aye,' she
said, 'thaa has?' So she put supper things away,
and then she and th' childer sat daan while th'

good man read a chapter i' God's Book ; then they all knelt together at the family altar, and committed their souls to the keeping of Him who never slumbers nor sleeps. In a little while after that they were all in bed and th' candle blown aat; they were just settling daan into sleep, when there came a loud knocking at th' front door, ran, tan, tan, tan. 'Ellow! who's there?' exclaimed th' good man of th' haase as he raised himself up in bed.

"'It's me!' answered a voice from th' aatside.

"'Me, who's me?'

"'I'm th' neighbour, thaa knaws.'

"'Aye, and a bonny neighbour thaa is to be comin' here knocking up sich a row at this toime o' th' noight.'

"'Why, I'm vary sorry,' chimes in th' voice aatsoide, 'vary sorry to trouble you, but a friend o' mine that's on a journey, has just come to aar haase, and wants his supper and a noight's lodgings, and we ha'nt a morsel o' bread to set before him, and I want to knaw if thaa'll lend us a loaf till my wife bakes.'

"'Get away hoam wi' the',' replied the man of th' haase. 'I'm i' bed, and canna be bothered; candle's aat, and we ha' no matches upstairs ; go home and come agean in th' mornin', and I'll lend the' some. Remember me to the' friend, goodnoight:' whereupon he shuffles daan into bed agean, and tries to compose himsen to sleep.

"But th' man aatsoide has been and fetched a big thick stick, and with this he starts to hammer th' door laader than ever, till he startles all th' sleepers in th' haase.

"'Naa then, what's th' matter?' shaats th' man from insoide, 'I thought thaa war gone hoam.'

"'Will thaa lend me a loaf till my wife bakes?' This was said in such a deliberate, determined voice, that the good man knows in a moment he won't be put off.

"'What thinks ta, lass? Mun I get up and gie him one? I don't believe he'll goa away; he'll bray t' door daan afore dayloight.'

"While th' wife is rubbing her eyes and hesitating a bit, th' man aatside rings sich a clash of bells on th' front door, as brought th' good man aat on th' floor in a twinkling.

"'Hold on! hold on, mon, I'm coming!' and he was off daanstairs to the cupboard like a shot, aat with a loaf, unlocked th' front door, handed forth th' bread to the man, who was just getting ready for another knock. 'I see,' said he, thaa weant be put off; tak' this, and go hoam wi' the'.'"

This story, told in the vernacular of the district, of which this is a very imperfect rendering, and accompanied with Abe's expressive gestures, was exceedingly effective, and not easily forgotten. Nor did he omit the beautiful moral of the parable, showing the necessity of prayer, importunate prayer, prayer at all times. "Keep knocking!" Abe would say, "God is only trying you a bit in not answering first knock; it's His way of proving whether you really mean it or not. Knock laader, pray on and on, He hears, He is coming, bless Him! He never said to th' seed of Jacob, 'Seek ye my face in vain.'"

"PUT UM ON THEESEN."

The Prodigal Son was a favourite subject with the "Little Bishop," and many are the quaint sayings which fell from his lips while dwelling on this interesting parable. The singular pictures which he drew of this young man in his degradation brought many a smile on the faces of the congregation. But his chief aim always was to get the youth back to his father's house again; here his emotions often overpowered him, and his joy was so great that he hardly knew what he was saying. Many of the friends still remember him on one occasion at Outlane. He had brought the poor prodigal to the top of a lane leading down to his father's house; there he stood, covered in rags and dirt, his head bare and his shoes gone; he is just timidly stopping at the corner of the lane debating whether he shall go on or turn back, when at that moment out comes the old man to look up and down the road; he sees that bit of human misery at the lane end, and in an instant recognizes him as his son, "'Mother! mother!' exclaims th' owd man, 'quick! quick! here's aar Jack standing at top o' th' loin. Oh, run! run my owd legs, tak' me to him! Here, Jack, my lad, come to me, the' father wants thee—come, come!' And in another moment the old man is hurrying with tottering steps and open arms towards his son, and folding him, rags and all, to his bursting heart." It was so real to Abe, and he was so carried away with the picture which was before his vivid imagination, that when he got the lad into the house, he exclaimed, "Put shoes on his hands, and rings on his feet,"—whereupon a brother in the chapel called out, "Nay, nay, Abe lad, thaa mun't put shoes on th' lad's hands, and th' rings on his feet; put um on roight, man." But Abe responded at the top of his voice, while tears came rolling over his face, "Put um on theesen and let me aloan! 'This, my son, was dead, and is alive again, he was lost and is faand!'" By that genuine burst of feeling, he reached a climax of eloquence that has seldom been surpassed in the history of preaching.

CHAPTER XVI.

"I am a Wonder unto Many."

SUCH were the words of David in olden times, and with propriety did "Little Abe" frequently adopt them in his day. Considering his condition prior to his conversion,—a wild, thoughtless, and wicked young man, having neither fear of God nor man before his eyes, and then contrasting it with what he had become by the grace of God; remembering his want of education, that he never could write, and by that means commit his thoughts to paper, and yet that his preaching was acceptable and profitable to the people, that he drew large congregations wherever he went, some people coming to hear him who seldom attended the places at any other time; that he was used by God in bringing many sinners into the fold of Christ, who are now useful members in the Church on earth, or enrolled among those who serve God in His temple in heaven, "Little Abe" really was " a wonder unto many."

A woman once said to him, "Aye, Abe, I like to hear the' preach."

"Bless th' Lord for that," responded Abe.

"But," continued she, "I many a toime wonders where thaa gets all th' sense from, and haa thaa foinds t' words to say, for thaa's niver been to college, nor ony place loike that."

"Who says I wor niver at college?" he replied. "I have been to a college where they mak' a roight job on um, woman."

"Why, what college hast ta been to? Not Ranmoor, I'll be baan?"

"Noa, not Ranmoor; it would puzzle th' Doctor to mak' onything o' me; I've been to th' fisherman's college, where Peter and th' rest on um went. I've learnt a bit at th' feet o' Jesus, bless Him!"

Yes, he had learnt to devote what little talent he possessed to the highest and happiest service in the universe, and his success as a labourer for Jesus shows that the great Master can make good use of any feeble instrumentality for the spread of truth and the salvation of mankind. "We have this treasure in earthen vessels that the excellency of the power may be of God and not of us," was a saying of apostolic days, but as true now as when uttered by St. Paul. When great scholars and brilliant orators or men of extraordinary natural and acquired parts become successful as the advocates of our Christian faith, there are always some more ready to pay a tribute to the

powers of these men, than to the Gospel which
they teach, ascribing their success not to the
inherent power of truth, but to the extraordinary
talent of its advocates. But when men like our
friend "Little Abe" are raised up for the Lord's
work, and the Gospel preached by them becomes
mighty in changing the hearts and lives of others,
these opponents of our blessed religion are at a
loss to find some human arm to which they can
ascribe the glory, and while they vainly seek such
arm, others can plainly see "that the excellency
of the power is of God, and not of us."

A great deal of the favour which "Little Abe"
met with was due to his *sincerity*. He was very
droll in his sayings; he was very original in his
manner of dealing out truth; his illustrations were
mostly drawn from things in everyday life which
everybody understood; his language was the plain
home-spun provincialism of the locality where his
hearers were born and brought up; but however
much may be due to these things, those who knew
him best would say, that his almost universal
acceptance was due to his undoubted sincerity.
This made everything he said in the pulpit quite
proper. What would appear out of place in any
other man, was becoming in him; all his odd sayings and gestures were kindly received, and never
an unpleasant feeling was excited in the breast of
any who really knew the man.

Oh, it is a grand thing when a man has so lived

and proved himself among those around him, that
they all feel his religion to be sincere! What good
may not such a man be capable of doing? He
may be unschooled and unread, he may be poor,
and hold but a humble position in the ranks of
life, and yet withal, he may exert a power which
neither rank nor learning can acquire, nor wealth
purchase. He rules hearts; learning may rule
heads, and wealth may influence manners, but
sincere goodness enshrines itself on the throne of
the heart.

Men among whom "Little Abe" lived and
worked, with whom he met from day to day,—
men who professed to have no regard for religion
as such, respected Abe's presence more than they
would that of their own fathers, and stopped their
unclean conversation at his approach, or by some
other unmistakable means indicated their deep
respect for him. They all knew what grace had
done for him, and they honoured the genuine
work, thereby entitling Abe to say, "I'm a wonder
unto many."

One man says, "If there were no other evidence
that religion is a good thing, there was proof
enough in Little Abe. I have had ample opportunities of watching his daily life for many years,
having worked in the same mill with him, and I
know what the other mill hands thought of him
as well ; everybody believed in the 'Little Bishop,'
and there wasn't a man to be found that would

utter a disrespectful word of him. He was often employed in what is called 'cuttling,' that is, drawing cloth from the machine. To do this he had to kneel on the ground ; it was easy work, and required very little thought. Many a time have I seen him, while in this position, praying and drawing off the cloth, and I have thought that Abe couldn't help praying if he got on his knees, whether it was in the mill or anywhere else.

"Sometimes on a Saturday the young people in the mill would say, 'Well, Bishop, where are you going to preach to-morrow ?' and then, with the brightest, kindest smile, he would tell them where his work for the next day lay, and perhaps he would ask them to go with him ; but on their refusing, he would add, 'Ah, my lads, yo' want your hearts changing by th' grace of God, and then yo' would be glad to run onywhere in His Name.' As years grew on him and he became infirm, I have seen him come into the mill on a Monday morning looking very tired, and I have said I thought he was working too hard on Sundays. 'Canna do that,' he would reply; 'I would do a thausand toimes maar for Jesus if I could ;" and then brightening up, he would add, ' I'd raather wear aat loike gooid steel, than rust aat loike owd iron ;' and he was true to his word ; he did wear out."

Many such testimonies might be added if it were necessary, all showing that religion in " Little

Abe" was the all-engrossing thing, but let this suffice. It is delightful to see how a good man may live in the midst of the ungodly, and keep his garments unspotted, and his name unsullied by the adverse influences around him. What a rebuke such a life is to many who excuse their looseness and irregularities because they are thrown among the irreligious; and how stimulative it becomes to others that are similarly situated, and trying to live consistently in the midst of all their evil surroundings!

CHAPTER XVII.

𝔄𝔟𝔢 𝔞𝔰 𝔞 ℭ𝔩𝔞𝔰𝔰 𝔏𝔢𝔞𝔡𝔢𝔯.

THE Class-meeting is one of the best institutions in Methodism. It has done as much as anything else, if not more, to keep up the spiritual life of the churches; it has been a refuge for tens of thousands of tempted ones; it has been a seasonable corrector to many who were just beginning to fall into the paths of sin, and has brought them back to Christ again; it has supplied the social need of our Christian faith, and gathered friends together for spiritual communion; it has been a safeguard against the devices of the devil by affording opportunities for the disciples of our Lord to compare their experiences, tell their temptations, and impart mutual encouragement to each other in the Divine life; it is a natural, seemly, and modest vent for the spiritual fire which glows and flashes in every heart that loves the Lord with sincerity. It was almost self-appointed; it came to be, or grew out of a class of circumstances which would at any other time have produced essentially the same thing; it is the outgrowth of the fervent piety which marked the lives of our fathers in the churches, and it has met the tendencies of glowing Christianity among us ever since. It is an encumbrance only where this kind of Christianity is not maintained; as godly zeal declines, so sinks the estimation for class-meetings; just as the appetite for food forsakes a sickly person, so the desire for experience meetings declines in a sickly church. Persons who never did attend class-meetings cannot be judged by them; their piety may deepen or diminish, but other tests must be found for them. The class-meeting is a Methodist gauge, and only here can it apply.

"Little Abe" was a class leader for many years, and there was no work more heartily enjoyed by him than this. The members of his class who survive him often talk of the grand times they had with the little man in this way; it was often like heaven on earth. He was a very successful leader, and always kept his members well together. If any of them absented themselves he was soon on their track, hunting them up and bringing them back to the fold.

"MY FATHER'S GOT PLENTY O' TIMBER."

His class was conducted in a neat little cottage near the chapel belonging to one of the members, who week by week opened his doors for the accommodation of Abe and his flock. Their meeting was held in a comfortable room which served the family as kitchen and parlour; here every Monday night the quaint old shepherd came to meet his sheep. The big family table was pushed back against the window, the elbow-chair was placed at the end for the leader, all the chairs and seats in the house were brought into this room and ranged around as conveniently as possible to accommodate the weekly visitors, and sometimes when this was done there were more people than seats, and the big table had to be drawn out again, and made use of as a resting-place for the homely people who gathered there; or a long board would be brought down from upstairs and its ends placed on two chairs, and thus an additional seat was extemporized.

This very board had the misfortune to snap in two one night while a brother was engaged in praying. He was a *powerful* man in prayer; his soul was inspired with zeal, and his body animated with strength, which on this occasion he vented in a succession of heavy blows on this devoted piece of timber, until suddenly it gave way with a loud crack and fell in two pieces on the floor, to the great discomfiture of those whose weight added to the strain. For some moments there was considerable confusion in the room, as may be supposed, and the praying was brought to a sudden halt, when

9

Abe's voice was heard above all, "Ne'er moind, lad, go at it! My Father's got plenty o' timber, and He'll send thee a new seat," whereon the meeting went on, as lively as before. Abe wouldn't allow any such trifles to interfere with the happy flow of feeling in his meetings; indeed, such incidents served rather to stimulate than abate the exuberance of his spirits. He knew that all things belonged to the Lord, and that He would make good all that was lost in His service, and therefore "he took joyfully the spoiling of his goods," and other folk's too. It is needless to say that the old seat was replaced by a new one.

"MY FATHER 'LL GIE THE' THIS HAASE" (House).

When Abe had been conducting his class for some years in the cottage before named, an event transpired which greatly disturbed his mind, and led him to fear he might have to remove his meeting to some other place. Now this was a sore trouble to him and to every one of his members; they had got accustomed to going there, and some of them had never met anywhere else, so that they could not bear the thought of being obliged to leave, yet there was some ground for the fear.

The person who owned the cottage was mother-in-law to the man by whom it was occupied; she died and left her property, which consisted chiefly of cottages, to be divided equally among her

children. Soon after the funeral the family met
in this very house to arrange the division of the
estate. The plan adopted was to draw lots for
houses, and as they were nearly of the same value,
this seemed equitable. So the lots were all prepared and placed together, and each person was
to draw one, and take the house named on the lot :
the drawing was to commence with the eldest, and
go down to the youngest. Now the wife of the
man in whose house the class met was the
youngest member of the family, and therefore
must take what all the others left. When everything was ready for the drawing to begin, the
proceedings were interrupted by a knock at the
door. The man of the house opened it, and found,
to his surprise, " Little Abe " there. " Come aat a
minute," said he, " I want to spaike to the'. On
getting outside Abe resumed, " I knaw what ye are
baan to do in there."

" Haa dost ta knaw ? " said the man.

" Ne'r moind, I knaw ; " and going close up to
his ear and placing his hand on the man's arm,
he said, " My Father 'll gie the' this haase, He
told me soa ; I've been to Him abaat it, and I
have His word on 't ; but afore thaa gets it, I want
the' to promise me that while I live I shall have my
meetin' here."

" Yo' shall," was the ready response ; " as long
as thaa and me lives this haase shall be oppen to
the' if we get it."

"Bless the Lord," said Abe, rubbing his hands, "I could loike to shaat" (shout) "but they'd hear me insoide. Ne'er moind, I knaw tha'll get it ;— gooid-noight!"

His friend then returned into the house, and immediately the drawing began. Each drew one lot ; then they all read them together, and as Abe predicted, the house in which they were assembled fell to the share of the man who lived in it. But this is. not the end of the story : it appears that one of the sons was not satisfied with his portion, and began to complain. The fact is he wanted this house, and if he had got it Abe and his class would have been turned out. So, rather than have any unpleasantness in the family, they all agreed to cast lots again and abide by the issue. This was done, and to the astonishment of all, this house fell a second time to the same man, and though it was considered the best lot, everyone felt it was fairly his, and he has it to this day.

It may suit some people to say this was a mere accident ; yes, just the same as the world is an accident and a thing of chance. Perhaps it was an accident, too, that "Little Abe" was able to foretell the issue of that lottery with such confidence, and was so eager to make his bargain for the use of the room before the lots were known. The *chance* that can show such intelligence, foreknowledge, and power, that can communicate its intentions beforehand, and afterwards verify them in this manner, has the attributes of God, and must be Divine; a *chance* that can hear and answer prayer, that can work out its own designs and baffle those of others, that can reveal secrets to His favourites and honourably keep covenants, deserves the faith and worship of all men : this was Abe Lockwood's God, and He shall be ours for ever and ever. There are some who say, " What is the Almighty that we should serve Him? and what profit shall we have if we pray unto Him ?" These scientific theorists and unbelievers are intensely anxious to prove that prayer is only wasted energy, that nothing can possibly come as direct answering to prayer, that if things do follow which seem to be in response to earnest and devout petition, they result from some other causes, which have no con-nection, except coincidental, with prayer.

Men who talk so don't pray, never did. They don't know what prayer is ; they are wrong in their first principles, and therefore all their deductions are awry ; it is impossible for anyone who dis-credits prayer to know what he is talking about. Prayer is a something going on within the soul, it is something which must be experienced to be understood ; and yet those who have no expe-rience presume to philosophize on the subject as if they had spent all their life in the exercise and study of prayer. Just as well might " Little Abe " try to talk scientifically, as those scientists speak on the merits or worth of prayer ; it is out of their sphere, they are out of their depth, and therefore it was a sad want of discretion which first tempted them to venture so far.

"Little Abe" was a much better judge of the value of prayer than these theorists ; he was much further learnt in this direction than any of them, and therefore his testimony was more reliable than theirs ; what to them was a mystery and impossibility was to him a simple daily enjoyment. They that would test the value of prayer *must really pray themselves*, and *believe* while they pray, otherwise they will be no wiser. Prayer is not disproved by the failure of improper petitions, but it is proved by the success attending supplications presented in the right spirit. If men expect nothing, they get what they expect, the Bible says so: "But without faith it is impossible to please Him : for he that cometh to God must believe that He is, and that He is a rewarder of them that diligently seek Him" (Heb. xi. 6).

Prayer was an exercise in which Abe was a proficient and spent much time; at his work he prayed, and in his chamber, long and earnestly, until he prevailed. Sometimes in the meetings, as Abe would say, "they gat agaat o' wrestling," and then he often became so importunate in his intercessions that his whole body prayed as well as his soul, and quite unconsciously he beat the bench at which he knelt, struck the floor with his clogs, sweat at every pore, and really wrestled with

God in mighty prayer, and then the glory was sure to come down and fill the place. Certainly at those times Abe and those who were with him were very noisy, and some who had no sympathy with anything of the sort, would make some disparaging remarks. There were some of old who would have silenced the loud cries of poor blind Bartimeus, but they could not, nor can they stop the voice of vehement prayer. Pray on, brethren, get hold of God, and then make what noise you like.

We want more of this praying spirit among the Lord's people, and less of the cold calculations of the unbeliever. Here lies the strength of the Christian Church, and not in its immense wealth, its high culture, its refined pulpit, or luxurious pew; it is that praying power which brings the Divine unction down. May God give us the praying power.

CHAPTER XVIII.

" Working Overtime.'

THE time came when "Little Abe" was much
sought after to speak at week-night meetings,
such as tea-meetings, missionary meetings, and the
like. It was considered a great point to have him
as one of the speakers; they were sure to have a
lively time if Abe came—for what with his own
original speech his running comments and responses while others were talking (a liberty which
every one allowed him), he kept the whole meeting
alive throughout.

This was what he called "working overtime." All
his Sundays were given, as a matter of course, to the
Lord's work, and the week-days to his daily calling; consequently what he did, in this way had to
be done at nights, after his day's work was finished.
Now as this kind of work grew upon Abe, there
were some who would tell him he was doing too
much, that he would injure himself; but he would

remind them that when he had to work at the
mill night after night, week after week, no one ever
thought of telling him he was doing too much.
"No," would be the response, "because you were
paid for that." Then Abe's soul was roused.
"Well, and does the' think my Father doesn't
pay me? Bless Him, He owes me nowt, He's paid
me double wages for every minute I have warked
for Him." And so he went on serving the Church
and honouring God to the utmost of his ability.

LITTLE ABE AND THE MULE.

He had a singular experience one dark rainy
night when going to a missionary meeting at
Shelley. He was late in arriving, so that the
meeting was somewhat advanced when he put in
an appearance. As he entered the chapel he was
greeted by a burst of clapping, and in a moment
every face brightened at the sight of him, though,
to tell the truth, he was rather unsightly, for he
was bedabbled with mud from his feet to his head,
and his big umbrella looked as if it had been on
the spree and rolled in the gutter; altogether he
appeared in unusual style for a public meeting.
It was no matter to him, however. He just shook
himself like a dog out of the water, placed his
bundle of whalebones and gingham in a quiet
corner, rubbed his numbed hands together, and
went smiling on to the platform. Nothing would
satisfy the people but that he should speak at once,

so he rose to his feet amid the hearty clapping of the whole audience, and said, "I niver knew so mich of th' trials of missionary wark in my loife as I do naa. I've been in trainin' for this meetin'. I've had to endure storms, rain, tempest, and dangers seen and unseen, for it wor that dark on th' road I could hardly see mysen, so, loike a returned missionary, I think I ought to let yo' knaw some'at abaat my trials." (Hear, hear.) "Well, yo' knaw, when I promised to come to this meetin', I meant being here somehaa, but I'av had a job. I thowt as I wor comin' I would mak' it as easy as I could for mysen, so I borrowed aar neighbour's mule. I didn't knaw mich abaat riding, so he telled me I wor to keep tight hold o' th' bridle, as th' owd mule had a way o' tumblin' fore'ards. Well, I gat on th' back wi' my umbrella oppen, for it wor pouring daan rain, and we set off, all three on us, umbrella, th' mule, and me. We gat on alroight most o' th' way. I had to scold th' owd animal sometimes, and tell him to get on or we'd be too late for th' meeting, so we kept gaining a bit o' graand by degrees, but troubles wor ahead. What wi' thinking abaat my speech and holding th' umbrella roight, I forgat to keep a toight hold o' th' bridle, and all at once th' mule tript, and th' umbrella and me went roight over his head into th' dike. I really wor astonished at mysen, and didn't know which to blame—th' mule or me. I think I ne'r gat off a cuddy so quick in my loife afore;

and th' owd mule would hardly understand me I
daresay, for he stopt in a moment and look'd over
at me as if he wor wondering if I always gat off in
that fashion. However, I soon scrambled aat o'
th' dike, and after a good bit o' trying I maanted
agean and set off on th' road; but I hadn't gone
far before I faan some'at wor wrang wi' th' bridle.
I couldn't guide th' beast roight somehaa, so I
felt abaat to try if I could foind aat what it wor,
and behold I had gotten th' bridle all on one soide.
Well, I dar'n't get off to set it roight, so I wor fain
to let th' owd beast goa his own gait till we gat to
Shelley."

The whole story was so amusing, and the more
so as told in Abe's inimitable style, that the people
laughed themselves into tears ; and yet they could
not but admire the zeal of the little man, and their
hearts warmed towards him, and to the missionary
cause as well, for as soon as Abe resumed his seat,
the chairman, who knew how to take the tide at its
flood, called for the collection to be made, and
there is no doubt it was a good one. Just at that
moment Abe shouted out, "Bless the Lord, I've
made th' collection speech to-noight."

A QUOTATION FROM SALLY.

At one of the meetings where "Little Abe " was
a speaker, he was exhorting the people to give
freely to the Lord's cause. "Some folk," he re-
marked, "say that Methodists are always after

money; well, we canna' do very mich withaat it, I wish we could, it's a deal o' bother, and takes sich a lot o' getting ; and yet it is a far worse job to be withaat ony." Then throwing his head over a little on one side he went on, " Aar Sally says money is th' rooit of all evil, but I says, 'Aye, lass, I knaw it ' wad be, if I wor to come home on Saturday withaat ony.'"

A LIST OF THE FAMILY NAMES.

At another meeting in which our little hero was speaking he got into an exceedingly happy mood, and was dwelling on the honour of being a child of God. His face shone with delight, his eyes glistened with joyful tears. " Bless the Lord," said he, " I'm a King's Son, and one of a royal line. Ah, and there are hosts maar in th' family besides me. Let's see," said he, " there's Jonathan Cheetham, King's Son ; there's James Crossland, King's Son ; there's James Carter, King's Son ; Glory ! there's Mary Carter, King's Son. Hallelujah!" How far he would have pursued the list of family names we don't know, had not the whole meeting burst into laughter and tears at Abe's unwitting mistake in calling Mary Carter a King's Son; but it was of no consequence to him ; a little slip of his happy tongue didn't mar his meaning ; the people cheered him, and on he went as blythe as ever.

It was reward enough for Little Abe to know that he had done his Master's work and brought

honour to His great name. The exertion which
these extra meetings entailed upon him, the long
weary marches out and home, were all performed
without a murmur or the slightest abatement of
zeal. He didn't serve the Lord with a footrule in
his hand, measuring and marking off to the eighth
of an inch. Abe strode over all narrow and stinted
measurements, and served his Master out of the
fulness of his warm and generous heart.

That miserable devotion which does as little as
possible for God, and magnifies that little into importance, Little Abe knew nothing about, and he
is a poor, pompous, pitiable thing that does ; the
open heart, the willing hand, the ready feet, are
among the few things that God Almighty is pleased
to see among His people ; the penitent that sheds
his tears by the dozen, the man that goes just the
length of his sixty-feet tape-measure and no more,
the champion that quenches his zeal in the first
obstacle that comes in his way, and turns back
from the fight, is unworthy the name and honour
of a Christian ; he is unfit to march in the glorious
succession of martyrs and confessors who follow a
Leader that dedicated His all to the world's welfare
and His Father's will. "For ye know the grace
of our Lord Jesus Christ, that though He was rich,
yet for your sakes He became poor, that ye through
His poverty might be rich."

CHAPTER XIX.

Methodist Lovefeast.

METHODISM has created new institutions and coined new words to express the object of them. The lovefeast is purely Methodistic: it is a meeting of Christian people belonging to one or more societies, where they relate their religious experience, and bear their testimony to the worth and influence of Divine grace in the soul.

Under the conduct of a minister, or someone duly appointed for the purpose, the meeting is opened with singing and prayer; then, while the people are sitting, bread and water are distributed to all present, to suggest that believers are members of one great family, and partners in the same spiritual provision made by Christ who gave Himself to be the Bread of Life for men. When this is done the offerings of the people are gathered, usually for the poor of the Lord's flock. The formalities ended, the meeting is thrown open for the relation of Christian experience, and any one speaks that is prompted.

In every period of Methodism the lovefeast has been a precious and popular means of grace. These meetings are held all through the country, every little church taking care to have its quarterly or annual lovefeast. And it is remarkable what a hold some of these meetings have upon the people; ten, or even twenty miles, have not been considered too great a distance to be travelled in order to be present at some of them, even though the entire journey has had to be performed on foot. Men and women, some of them stricken in years and bowed down with the toils and cares of a long and hard life, have joyfully walked many a weary mile for the pleasure of attending a lovefeast; old people, leading their grand-children by the hand, and telling them of the stirring times of early Methodism; younger people in groups, singing revival hymns as they plod steadily along the dusty or miry roads under melting sun or pelting rains, making their way to these attractive and soul-stirring meetings, contending against every obstacle and overcoming every hindrance, determined to be there and do honour to the Divine Master, who said, "Ye are my witnesses."

There have been some of the grandest manifestations of Divine power at these gatherings, as seen and felt in the sweet, gentle, and unconscious melting of feelings, until the whole congregation has been broken down to tears and songs of joy and praise; or coming suddenly upon them as a "rushing mighty wind," without sound or sign, save in the bending of heads, the breaking of hearts, the streaming tears, and the adoring responses of the people. Then, believers have caught the spark of sanctifying fire from God Himself, and declared it; then, men have been endued with the gift of tongues, and spoken with apostolic power; then, sinners, drawn into the place by the peculiar attractions of the occasion, have felt their souls shaken by Divine energy, like forest trees in a tempest, and trembling, bending, rending, breaking, have fallen in the storm of Heaven's mercy, and cried for help and found it. Oh, how many there are now in glory or on the way, of whom it may be said, "Convicted in a lovefeast! converted in a lovefeast! sanctified in a lovefeast!" Their name is "legion, for they are many." Hallelujah!

Some things among the usages of the churches we may perhaps afford to dispense with and suffer no loss, but not this glorious means of grace. If in any place they have lost their power, the fault is not in the institution, but in the Church; religious declension is the greatest enemy to this good old custom. If the Lord's people return to their first love, the lovefeast will resume its former glory and power. Oh, Lord, "wilt Thou not·revive us again, that Thy people may rejoice in Thee?"

Methodism cannot afford to forsake her old ways

for new and untried ones; they are intelligent,
proper, and essentially Christian. Lovefeasts are
the olive branch which we have received from the
revered hands of our fathers and mothers in the
faith, not to be cast away, but to be prized and kept
as a mark of our love for them, for each other,
and for Christ our Saviour; and though the green
branch which they left us may be somewhat faded,
and its leaves droop in our moistureless hands,
though it has lost some of the freshness it had
when it first came to our keeping, thank God!
thank God! it is not dead, it lives! and can be
revived. It wants more moisture; sprinkle tear-
drops of penitence upon its shrunken foliage; let
the springs of our sympathy once more flow over
it; let us ask God to give us the "upper and the
nether springs," that *His* love and ours may flow
out in one united stream; let us come to that
stream, near, nearer, to the brink, and olive branch
in hand, plunge in, refresh ourselves, and revivify
the blessed, beautiful, and sacred symbol.

There was no meeting in which Little Abe was
more at home than a lovefeast; whether as con-
ductor or in a private capacity,—if such a term can
be applied to Abe,—he gloried in a rousing lovefeast. His love for these meetings and his aptitude
in conducting them occasioned a great demand for
his presence. He had such a way of interspersing
enlivening comments between the speakers. He
was a good singer, too, and was always ready with

some hymn expressive of the feeling of the meeting. Then he had the power to make everyone feel at home, so that he was the very man to lead a love-feast, although he did sometimes say things that would shock very orderly and circumspect persons.

DEVIL DIDN'T POP THEE.

Little Abe was leading a lovefeast in Berry Brow Chapel ; the place was crowded, people had come from far and near; the Holy Spirit was present in great power ; there was no lack of witnesses, two or three being often on their feet together waiting for an opportunity to speak. Little Abe, as he said, "was fair swabbing o'er," he wept for joy.

A young man at length rose to relate his Christian experience. He had but lately been converted to Jesus, and before that had been a very wicked, drunken, degraded character. He proceeded to say what the Lord had done for him, how He had found him in his sins and misery, and taken hold of him when hardly anyone else would look at him, except a policeman, who felt as if he had a sort of right to him, and often found him board and lodgings for a few weeks. At the time of his conversion he was almost naked, and absolutely destitute ; said he, "I had popt" (pawned) "my coat, and popt my shoes, my vest, my shirt, and every-thing on which I could raise money, and I was almost in hell." This was more than Abe could sit under ; he sprang to his feet and exclaimed,

"It's a rare job th' devil didn't pop thee and all, my lad! Praise th' Lord!" The young man fell on his seat and vented his gratitude in a fresh burst of tears, and many an eye in that meeting ran over as well.

RELIGION ALL HUMBUG.

Little Abe once got up in a lovefeast. "Friends," said he, "a man asked me what I made so mich noise abaat religion for; he said, 'It's all humbug,' and I said, ' Thaa'rt roight for once, mon ; it's th' sweetest humbug that iver I tasted. I have been sucking it for mony a lang year, and it is sweeter than iver.'" (Humbug is the Yorkshire name for sweets and goodies). It was just in Abe's way to turn the tables on his assailant, and certainly in this case the Little Bishop had the best of the encounter, and the joy of the humbug as well.

PENITENT PHYSIC.

The Bishop was leading a lovefeast in Shelley Chapel (where it is said that the Rev. John Wesley once preached), and one of the speakers had been a backslider, but had determined to return to the Lord. This man was telling the meeting his bitter sorrow, and how he had drunk of the wormwood and gall of repentance, and as he spoke tears ran chasing each other down his face. " Bless th' Lord," said Little Abe, " I see my Father has been

giving the' some penitent physic, and it's made the'
'een" (eyes) "run. Ne'er moind, lad, He'll heal
thee heart, and wipe 'away all tears from thee 'een.'"

HONLEY FEAST MONDAY.

The Honley feast is one of the remaining relics
of byegone times, and is tenaciously kept year by
year throughout the parish as a holiday. It begins
with Sunday, and extends over the greater part of
the week, during which time the people enjoy
themselves in ways suited to their varied tastes,
too many of them indulging in the cup which
brings aching heads and empty pockets. What a
pity it is that men, and even women, too, are so
infatuated as to think that pleasure can only be
found in drunkenness and public-house brawling!
Thank God there are many who know the folly of
this, and have other and better ways of finding
pleasure. Ever since Salem Chapel was first
built it has been the custom to hold a lovefeast
there on Honley Feast Monday, and this is perhaps
the most popular meeting in the whole year, and
is always looked to with great interest. People
come to this lovefeast from many miles around,
and the chapel is invariably filled to overflowing.

This was always a great occasion with Little
Abe—a real red letter day. I remember attending
this annual meeting some years ago. Abe was
there, and he certainly monopolised a good share
of my attention. He was very happy, and kept on

ringing changes with clapping, stamping, shouting,
and sometimes, when under strong feelings, he
pealed a clash altogether, with hand, foot, and
voice. "Hey, lads!" he said, "it's grand! it gets
better and better, bless th' Lord!" His face was
covered with smiles from his smooth chin to his
bald forehead; he never ceased smiling during all
that service,—for no sooner had his joyous countenance spent itself on one pleasant thing, and the
light, dancing ripples begun to subside, than something else presented itself to his notice, and another
smile passed across his face like a playful breeze
over a clear pool, shaking up the waves again; and
so on he went, through all that service, with a face
as bright as a sunbeam.

At length Abe rose to his feet, still smiling, and
his hands clasped together; every eye was on him
in a moment, and smiles and tears of joy mingled
all over the chapel; the women wiped their eyes,
and the men shouted, "Glory, Abe! God bless
the', lad." "Friends," he began, "I am happy, I
mun spaike naa, or I'st brust mysen." "Go on,
Abe," came from all parts of the chapel. "Hey,
my lads, I mean to go on; I'm noan going to turn
back naa; it's heaven I set aat for, and heaven I
mean. I've been on th' road aboon fifty years, and
I'st get t' th' end afore lang." And then he went
on to say how glad he was to see them there once
more, and to see the place full of earnest wor-
shippers. "You knaw it warn't always soa. I can

remember when we wor just a few, but we agreed to pray for a revival, and gie th' Lord no rest until we should mak' His arm bare amang us. We started a prayer-meeting on Sunday mornings at five o'clock to th' minute, and they that worn't there at time should be locked aat. Well, yo' know, I wor' baan to be at that meeting. So I telled aar Sally on Saturday noight I mun be up i' th' morning at half-past four. Well, wod yo' believe it, I waked abaat five minutes to five. I wor aat o' bed in a wink, and shoved my feet in my stockings, and then on wi' my breeks, scratted up my booits" (boots) "i' my hand, and off I ran in my stocking feet. When I gat hoalf-way up th' Braa th' clock struck five, and I pushed one fooit in my booit, fastened up my gallasses, and ran on agean panting up th' hill, and just as I came t' th' gate I saw th' chapel door shut in my face, so I wor locked aat; but I wor noan baan to looise my meeting. While they insoid wor getting ready, I finished dressing mysen. By-and-bye I hears one on 'em give aat a hymn, and I clapped my ear t' th' key-hoil and listened for th' words, and then I put my maath to th' hoil and sang with 'em, and so I kept on until they began to pray. Then I listened, and shaated Amen through th' hoil, and kept on while iver they prayed. At last my owd friend Bradley stopped in th' middle of his prayer,—'Oppen that door,' he said, 'I canna pray with that chap shaating in at th' key-hoil that road;' so they oppened th' door, and I went in and had my meeting after all,—but yo' moind I wor nivcr late agean."

Our little friend will be remembered as a love-feast man for many years to come. His name had quite grown to be associated with the Conference lovefeast of the Methodist New Connexion, and many are the affectionate references to our brother in these grand annual gatherings even to this day. His voice is not now heard as it once was, along with that of Thomas Hannam, John Shaw, and men of like spirit and notoriety; but his name is still fragrant in the affectionate memories of those who are in the habit of attending our Conference lovefeast.

"BREED 'EM YOURSENS."

Although Little Abe was no narrow-minded sectarian, he still loved to foster in the minds of his own children a preference for the people that had, under God, saved his soul, and made him what he was, and he tried to bind his family to the Church of his choice. Spending a Sunday in the town of Dewsbury, in company with a devoted brother and local preacher who is now in heaven, they were led to converse about the Community to which they both belonged. Abc said, "I was born in th' New Connexion, never aat of it, and by God's help I'st die in it, and I hope my children after me." And then, taking up an incident which his own words had called to mind, he said, " My lad went by a cheap trip to Hull t'other day, and what dost ta think wor th' first thing he axed for when he gat there?" "Don't know," replied his friend. "Why, afore he gat aat at station yard, he goes up to a man and says, 'Can yo' tell me th' way t' th' New Connexion Chapel?' Naa," he added, looking across at his friend; "if yo' want th' roight soort, yo' mun breed um yoursens;" a saying which, put into other words, simply means that if we are to have reliable members in the Church, pious parents must bring in their own children, and let them grow up in the fear of the Lord and love of His people, and the maxim is correct.

CHAPTER XX.

𝔓𝔞𝔱𝔦𝔢𝔫𝔱 𝔦𝔫 𝔗𝔯𝔦𝔟𝔲𝔩𝔞𝔱𝔦𝔬𝔫.

A BE LOCKWOOD had to encounter many troubles arising from a variety of causes, but that which seemed to harass him most was poverty. Having a large family to bring up, and earning but moderate wages by his employment, his head was seldom above water ; he just managed to keep above the drowning point. Only the brave, honest, and godly poor who have struggled through similar difficulties, can really know what that good man and his wife had to contend against in this way.

Yet how. often do we find poverty and piety yoked together in one house. What a mercy it is that piety will condescend to dwell with poverty ; sit down at the same dry crust, or sit without it ; wear the same patched and threadbare raiment, and not complain ; stay in the same circle, endure the same hunger, cold, sickness, and suffering with unmurmuring constancy, and taking more than half the load of trouble on her own neck will sit the long night through, and "sing of mercy" till the day breaks, and the light comes, and the sun shines again. "Godliness with contentment is great gain."

How many of the Lord's jewels have been ground, cut, and polished on the wheel of poverty ; polished, but not set, for poverty is neither the gold nor silver for the setting. No matter, God does not care for the setting, it is the diamonds He loves, " and they shall be mine, saith the Lord of hosts, in that day when I make up my jewels."

When, however, industry, economy, and patient courage had done all, poor Abe was sometimes almost overwhelmed by hardships,—almost, but not altogether. He had a firm faith in God, and used to say, " My Father knows haa mich I can carry to a grain, and He wean't lay a straw too mony upon me, bless Him." In the midst of all the little Bishop maintained a happy heart and a cheerful countenance ; he made as little of his poverty as some people do of their luxuries, and an ordinary observer might have supposed he never had a sorrow, or felt a care. The fact is he did not hoard his troubles as some persons do ; he did not like them well enough for that. They hung very loosely about him at any time, and he shook them off as soon as he could ; instead of buttoning them up in his breast, and keeping them until they rankled, festered, or turned sour, he loosened his bands, bared his bosom to the first healthy breeze of joy that blew, and laughed the moment his sorrows were gone.

"WATTER GRUEL."

He was one day walking several miles to a preaching appointment, in company with another brother who was going to the same place. On the way his friend's nose began to bleed, and they had to stop, though the man's nose still kept on bleeding. Abe tried to stop it : he put a cold stone to the man's neck, held his arms up over head, and resorted to a variety of acknowledged remedies, but with very little effect. "What mun I do, Abe?" said the man. The little Bishop thereupon proceeded to give him his advice. "I'll tell the' what to do," said he ; "thaa mun strike at th' rooit" (root) "o' th' evil ; thaa lives o'er high ; thaa should try watter gruel for six weeks, and thaa'd cure that nose, that's haa I do." A burst of laughter from both hastened the cure, and on they went again with the journey. There was in this quaint remark of his just the slightest reference to the poor fare on which he had many a time set out on a long journey and a hard day's work in the cause of his Divine Master; often enough dear old Abe was like brave Gideon of old, "faint, yet pursuing."

He used to say when he met people who carried their troubles in their faces, "Yo' ha' no need to pull such lang miserable faces, raand 'um up a bit!

What! are yo' gotten on dark soid o' th' hedge?
Yo' mun flit into th' sunshine, there's plenty o'
room." And what a blessing it would be if people
who nurse their sorrows would begin to count and
cherish their joys instead ; the world, and especially
the Church, would be full of bright faces and happy
hearts.

THE HALLELUJAH COAT.

There was a time when Little Abe was badly
provided against the cold, wet, inclement weather
which he had to encounter in the work of the Lord,
and coming out of the chapels on winter nights
exposed him to many a dangerous chill. His only
extra covering was a thick woollen muffler around
his neck, yet in this way he bore uncomplaining
the brunt of storm and pelt of rain. One Sunday
night after the little Bishop had been preaching, a
man came and invited him to supper before starting
for home, and he went. Supper over, Abe prepared
to be off; it was a bitter night, cold and wet. On
seeing him about to start, the good man said, " I've
got something for you, Bishop." Abe looked round
and saw him standing with a big, thick overcoat
open, ready for him to put on. Without a word of
remark he thrust his arms into the coat, and his
host proceeded to button it up from his throat to
his heels, smiling all the time; this done, he stood
back to look at him. Abe clapped his hands together, and shouted "Hallelujah! hallelujah!! I

can say now't else—hallelujah ! a top coit ! a hallelujah coit !" And away he went out into the
darkness and rain shouting, " A Hallelujah top
coit ! " That garment was always known after as
" the hallelujah coit."

TEMPTED OF THE DEVIL.

Every Christian knows something of the wiles
of the devil, and how busily he goes about to tease,
annoy, and break the peace of the Lord's people.
Abe had many a tussel with this enemy, but in
the strength of faith and prayer he conquered him.
During the early years of Abe's Christian life the
devil often endeavoured to raise doubts in his
mind on fundamental truths ; but Abe was not to
be moved from the faith. What he could not
understand nor explain, he yet believed with all his
heart, so that in time the enemy yielded every
point of dispute up to him, and Abe kept his heart
in perfect peace, so far as these things were con-
cerned. If Satan came to him, it was generally
on some unimportant thing which might harass
and divert from better things. Abe would say,
" Th' owd enemy 's ge'en o'er playing ' th' roaring
lion,' and turned into a flee, running and hopping
all o'er me." And thus the devil would sometimes
assail him, rousing his feelings, exciting his imagination and anger, and kindling his resentment to
a pitch that sometimes made Abe almost ashamed
of himself, especially as it was all about nothing.

ACCUSED OF SWEARING.

After preaching one Sunday at Wellhouse, a place about four miles from where he resided, he was making his way home in the cool of the summer evening, and had got within a very short distance of Berry Brow. Following on the same road was a man that knew Abe very well, who was trying to overtake him. As this man drew nearer he heard the Bishop talking rather loudly, and giving expression to some very extraordinary language, accompanied by sundry violent flourishes of his walking-stick and stamping of his foot, and the man was amazed as he heard Abe break out, "Thaa 'rt a liar, thaa owd devil!" A few moments' silence followed this outburst, during which the little man was walking like a champion racer; then suddenly he broke out again, "I tell the' thaa 'rt a liar, and I will n't believe a word on 't." Then followed another brief silence, and then another excited explosion, which brought Abe to a standstill. "Didn't I tell the' I don't believe the'? Away with the', thaa lying old devil!"

By this time the man came up to him and said, "Why, Abe, whatever art ta swearing abaat soa on a Sunday noight?"

"Swearing! me swearing!" exclaimed Abe. "I'm noan swearing, my lad."

"But I yeerd the' mysen."

"When?"

"Naa, this minute; thaa called somebody a lying owd devil, and sich loike."

"Oh," said the little Bishop kindling at the sudden recollection of what had been passing in his mind, " I've left my Sunday pocket-handkerchief in th' pulpit at Wellhaase, and th' owd devil wor telling me aar Sally wod scold me, and I told him him he wor a lying owd devil, and so he is ; but I didn't knaw onybody could yeer me." In this way the enemy assailed him on his way home from his pious work, grudging him the peace of mind which a good man has in the service of his Master. Satan would not raise any vital point of faith or duty with Abe, because he knew he would be beaten, and Abe would be blest, and would rise high on the wings of his faith out of the devil's reach ; but he could spring a snare upon the good man about his pocket-handkerchief, and gradually worry and tease him into a conflict until he forgot altogether the thought of better things.

COUNTING THE ORGAN PIPES.

Another amusing story is told of Little Abe, showing how Satan sometimes succeeded in trailing a false scent across his path, and leading his mind astray for a time, or, so to speak, shunting him on to a siding, and keeping him there until he dis-covered the snare. He was sitting in Berry Brow Chapel listening, or endeavouring to listen, to the preacher ; it was soon after the new organ was introduced into that place of worship. Abe sat just opposite the organ, so that he could not avoid seeing it. Several times during the service the little Bishop had fidgeted about, and indicated signs of impatience from some cause or another ; when all at once, to the astonishment of preacher and people, Abe exclaimed, "I tell the' there's soa many pipes in that organ, I've caanted 'em a dozen times already ; if thaa doesn't believe it, caant 'em theesen, devil."

We may imagine the effect produced by Abe's outburst of indignation, that the devil should doubt the accuracy of his counting in a matter so trivial, as well as the annoyance and shame he felt that he had allowed his old enemy to make a dupe of him again. Yet it is only an illustration of the insignificant things that serve to call off our minds from the pursuit of holy studies. The devil would dispute through a whole service about a couple of flies, rather than permit a saint to wait upon God without distraction. It shows that we need to be very watchful against the influence of that arch enemy, even in the Lord's house.

Little Abe, with all his excellences, had his infirmities like other men, and he felt them keenly. It was a cause of great grief to him when, through unwatchfulness, he was led into folly. "Could ye not watch with me one hour?" was said to the weary disciples of old, and might often be repeated to the Lord's people to-day. "Watch, therefore, lest ye enter into temptation."

An Evil Temper.

One source of temptation to Little Abe was his temper; and yet here few would think he had any trouble at all. If people who knew him were canvassed on this question, the uniform testimony would be that he had a most even disposition; few could be found to testify that they ever saw him overcome by anger. He was, however, naturally of a quick, sensitive temper, and had to keep a jealous watch upon himself, in order to hold this tendency in subjection; the consequence was that it seldom gained the mastery over him after his conversion. Grace turned the lion into a lamb, and subdued the evil spirit within him, and as he grew in grace, the marks of the old Adam became less distinct. Still it was always an occasion for prayer and watchfulness with him; he would not allow himself to be tempted from this side of his character, if he could avoid it. Should anything transpire which was likely to rouse the evil spirit, Abe would take his hat and run away, rather than let the enemy gain ascendancy over him; he felt that it was often better to " hide than 'bide."

All our readers may not be troubled with a fiery temper, but they who are should watch it closely, or they will burn themselves. If you have fire about, keep powder and petroleum out of the way, or there may be an explosion ; he that tempts the fire with combustibles must surely pay the penalty sometimes. The safest and wisest policy is to put the fire out altogether ; get the evil temper destroyed by Divine grace, and then this "sin shall have no dominion over you."

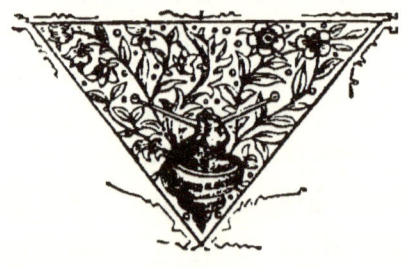

CHAPTER XXI.

"The Liberal Debiseth Liberal Things."

LITTLE Abe was endowed with a generous
heart, but with very limited means. He
could generally say as the Apostles did to the
lame man, "Silver and gold have I none, but
such as I have give I thee;" yet he often devised
means whereby he could enjoy the luxury of
giving to others. His own children, and even
those of the village, knew they could get a penny
from Abe if he had one in his pocket, although it
might be the last he had in the world, and many
a time he might be seen surrounded by a swarm
of children in the street, all begging sweets or
some other little trifle of him ; and you want no
better proof of a man's habitual kindness than to
see him often beleaguered by little children : they
only beg where they get something.

If any poor neighbour was in want, and Abe
had any means of assisting him, he would not wait

to be asked. Many a time he has gone home to
Sally and told her of some poor creatures who
had no bread in the house, and then he would
wind up his tale of sorrow with, "Naa, lass, we'll
be loike to tak' 'em a loaf," whereupon the good
woman would go to the cupboard and take out a
big family loaf, and hand it to him, and he would
hurry away to gladden the hearts of the hungry
children.

People do not need to be rich to exhibit the
spirit of true generosity, because it is not so much
in the amount given, as in the spirit in which it
is done, and the sacrifice involved in the act. It
is a truly noble thing for a wealthy man to bestow
of his abundance on the needy around him, and
he who does so is sure to gain a place in the affections of the people. Everyone admires a liberal
man ; indeed, it is questionable whether admiration
for this quality may not sometimes blind us to
other things in the same persons which are actual
faults, and hence a man may be intemperate or
profane or worldly, and people say, "Well, but he
is such a generous fellow," and that is taken as
mitigation of his faults : thus he is allowed to
indulge in many wrongs, because he has one excellency in his character. Men are not often impartial
judges ; their minds are warped by unduly regard-
ing one virtue more than another, and consequently
their verdict on character is not always reliable.
Give a benevolent man his full meed of honour,

but let not his liberal gifts become the purchase price at which he may obtain indulgence for other sins, or he makes morality only a mockery.

Generosity is an essential mark of the Christian character, and should display itself in every follower of our Lord. This is the spirit which prompted the poor of the Lord's flock to share their scanty means among their poorer brethren, and therefore, though Abe Lockwood was never in his life worth many shillings at one time, he was one among a multitude of humble and generous spirits moving in the lower walks of life, who often enjoy the pleasure of relieving the wants of sufferers around them.

"A Good Name is Better than Great Riches."

Among the people in his own locality no one stood in better repute than Little Abe. If any sick person wanted spiritual direction or comfort they would send for Little Abe. He was quite at home in the sick-room; the sight of his bright genial face would be sure to cheer the sufferer: and then he knew so well how to lead the penitent sinner to the Saviour, that the gloom of many a bedside has been dispelled by his humble ministrations in this way.

He loved this work, and gave a great amount of his spare time in visiting the sick. He was ready to go anywhere, any time, night or day, that he might help to sustain the soul in the last trial of faith ; and many an hour has he sat by the bed-side of some dying neighbour, talking, singing, praying, and trying to cheer him through the valley of death.

The little Bishop was general religious factotum in his own village, and especially among those who were in any way connected with Salem Chapel. In baptisms and burials he was held by many in as high repute as the regular ministers. Often it happened that he was fetched by some troubled parent to baptize a dying child, and he would perform the rite with as great satisfaction to the friends, in his blue smock and clogs, as he could have done had he worn the white neckcloth, and passed through ordination honours.

"WILT TA KNUG ?" (KNEEL).

A man came one evening to Abe's house, knocked at the door, then opened it a little way, thrust in his face and said, "Is Abe in?" It was a most unusual thing to see that man there, for he was a wicked, drunken character, a trouble to the neighbourhood where he lived, and often a terror to his poor wife and children. Many a time Abe had tried to induce him to go to the Lord's house and begin to lead a new life ; but sin had such a hold upon him that he only made light of everything good, and, in his ignorance and hardihood, professed to disbelieve in God and His Word.

" Is Abe in ? " asked the face at the door.

"Yes, I'm here," replied the little man in question, looking up from his Bible, and peering over the lamp on the table to see who the speaker was. "Come in, mon ; open th' door and come in."

And in a little further came the face and head, followed by a pair of broad shoulders and a huge body, whereupon Abe saw who they belonged to, and rising from his seat he noticed that the great hard face was clouded and softened with sorrow. Ah, it is a hard heart that does not melt sometimes.

" What's ta want ? " asked Abe, in a kind tone.

" Arr bit bairn 's badly," replied the big man, "and th' missus wants the' to come and sprinkle it."

" Th' missus want me does she,—and what does thaa want ? " said Abe, looking meaningly at him· " Does thaa want me to come ? "

" Ay," responded the man, looking rather humble, and feeling that Abe had obtained his first victory by that confession.

" Well, I'll goa wi' the'," and, putting on his hat, they went out together, and betook themselves to the dwelling of the visitor. Arriving there Abe beheld a painful yet by no means uncommon picture. A room miserably furnished, and not the ghost of comfort anywhere ; several little ragged children stood grouped together, and in the midst of them was the saddest figure of all—"the missus," the wife, the mother, in tears, and on her lap, wrapped in an old faded shawl, was a dying infant. The woman tried to smile amid her tears as Abe came in, just the shadow of a smile, and then her poor face settled again to that look of anguish it had before, as if all her meagre joy were slowly dying with that little creature that lay feebly gasping on her lap. It was so like a woman to remember amid her grief, to give a sign of welcome to her visitor.

"Aye, my lass, I'm real sorry for the'; thaa has a mother's heart, I see, and thaa'd loike to keep thee bairn, I knaw thaa wad; but thaa mun remember God has first claim on 't, and if He wants it, thaa'll be loike to let Him ha' it. He can tak' better care on 't nor thaa can; bless it, it'll sooin be better off nor ony on us—don't fret, my lass—th' Lord comfort the'." And so in this way Little Abe went on talking, softening, comforting, and strengthening the bitter heart of that poor woman; at length he said, "Thaa wants me to baptize th' little un, I reckon."

"If yo' pleeas," she replied. "Jack," added she turning to her husband, who stood all the time with his back to the table, trying hard to keep his eyes dry and swallow down a lump that was continually rising into his throat, "get a basin o' watter, my lad." It was said so sadly and yet so kindly, that if Jack had had to go through fire to fetch that basin of water he would have got it. In a minute or two he came with the basin in his big broad hand

and stood close up to his wife's side, looking down
on his dying child.

"This is a religious service," said Abe, "and I
want yo' to understand that." He had his doubts
about the man, notwithstanding his evident effort
to control his emotions ; he knew the man's sinful
character, knew his hostility to everything religious,
and now that he had him to something like an
advantage, he wanted to make the most of it.
"I'm baan to baptize that bairn in God's name,
and we mun kneel daan and pray for it ; " and
then looking at the father he said, " Wilt' ta knug "
(kneel) "daan with us ? "

The man made no answer, but still kept by his
wife's side, looking down on the infant.

" Wilt ta knug with us, Jack ? " he repeated; "it's
thy bairn, and it'll sooin be gone." Still there came
no reply; a conflict was going on in the breast of
that strong man, the wicked man of the world was
contending against the father.

"If thaa will n't knug beside the' wife and
bairns, I'll go haam agean," said Abe.

The man was conquered ; the devil was strong
in him, but the father was stronger. He could not
bear the thought of paying a slight to his dying
child. "I'll knug," said he, and that instant he
fell on his knees. Abe baptized the child, and
then all of them knelt together, while he poured
out his soul in earnest supplication to God for the
child and the family ; but especially for the father

who was now, almost for the first time in his life, found humbly kneeling at the throne of grace. It would have been very gratifying if we could say that this was the turning-point in that man's life ; but here our knowledge of the case ends. It is, however, not too much to hope that the memory of that sad night, coupled with the loss of the little child, would have a good influence on the subsequent life of the man, and perhaps be the means, under God, of leading him to seek that grace which alone could afford him hope of meeting his child again in the kingdom of glory.

Whether this was so or not, the incident shows the high esteem in which Little Abe was held by the people among whom he lived. We see that he gained a decided advantage over the hardened sinner when he constrained him to kneel before the Lord ; and it also shows that when scoffers and so-called unbelievers are brought into the shadows of death, their unbelief forsakes them, and like devils, "they believe and tremble."

It was no uncommon thing for Abe to be called out of the mill to conduct the burial service at Salem, in place of the minister, who perhaps had never been informed of the funeral, or even of the death. No matter, poor man, he has sadly lowered himself in the opinion of the family and friends by not being present. He might have known he would be wanted, and at what time of the day, and in what place, and it is very unkind of him

not to be there. Where is he? Poor innocent, he
is tramping off to a distant country appointment
in simple ignorance of the misdemeanour of which
he is guilty. A minister ought to know everything
—know who is well and who is not; ministers are
different from all other people, and more is
expected from them. If, for instance, any one is
ill, the doctor must be sent for; but the minister
is expected to come without being requested. It
is his duty to attend to the sick of his flock. It
is no matter whether he knows of the illness or
not, he ought to know of it; a pretty shepherd he
must be not to know if any of his sheep are ill;
he should make inquiries for himself among the
people. Are any persons dead here, or any sick?
any to be prayed for? or are there any disaffected
parties waiting to be coaxed into a good humour?
any croakers in want of a good subject to vent
their bile upon? or anything at all in the general
ministerial way that wants doing? A man could
easily find out what is going on, and what is going
off, with a little ingenuity and perseverance; and
it would save all the trouble and expense of a post
card to the minister asking him to call. Let us
hope, therefore, that in future there will be no
misunderstanding upon these important matters,
because every place in the land is not favoured
with such an able, willing, and acceptable substitute
as the people of Berry Brow had in Little Abe.

Reference has already been made to the esteem

with which he was regarded by his fellow-work-people. As years went on this regard was, if possible, intensified, and it was beautiful to see how the younger men in the mill would strive to lighten his work, and make his duties as easy for him as possible. Nor was this kindly feeling confined to the mill operatives ; his masters, gentlemen of high position in the locality, held him in great esteem, for they knew him to be a honest, upright man, and a faithful servant. He had, in his latter days, many liberties and favours which could not be permitted to their employés generally ; often one or another of his masters would come into the mill, and have a few minutes' conversation with him about his work as a preacher, and his religious zeal, enlivened by his irrepressible humour, almost invariably sent the master away with his face covered with smiles, and his good opinion of the Little Bishop confirmed.

CHAPTER XXII.

Used Up.

AS time went on, and year after year was added to his age, Little Abe began to show, by unmistakable signs, that he was becoming an old man ; and although his lively temperament enabled him to hold up against his infirmities for some time, the day came when he confessed he was an old man and stricken in years ; he began to speak of himself as being "used up," "worn aat," "done for," and the like. All the marks were upon him ; his hair was snowy white, his face was furrowed with age, his sight was dim, his step was slow and feeble, his voice tremulous, and the signs were plainly seen that the Little Bishop was drawing near the end of his journey.

One day he was unexpectedly called to go into his master's office, and immediately he made his way there, when something like the following dialogue took place. "Well, Abe," his master

began, " I am sorry to observe that you are getting
so infirm that you cannot do a day's work now. I
have seen this for some time, yet did not want to
turn you away, but now I am sorry to say you will
have to leave the mill, and I must put another man
in your place."

This coming so suddenly from the master was
enough to stagger a stronger man than Abe, and
certainly he felt a little troubled at what he had
heard, but he could put his trust in God.

" I'm vary sorry to laave, maaster, but I knaw I
am gettin' owd and used up."

" And what will you do for a livelihood, Abe?
I'm afraid you would not be likely to get employment anywhere else at your age, what will you do?"

" Well, I don't knaw what I mun do, but I'm
sure my Father will niver see me want; ' I have
been young and now am old, yet have I never
seen the righteous forsaken or his seed begging
bread.'" This beautiful triumph of simple faith in
God was soon followed by its reward; his master
had carried the test far enough, he saw once more
his old servant was a man of God, his face broke
out into a smile which showed he had only been
playing with Abe: " We have arranged to give
you a weekly allowance sufficient to keep you and
your wife as long as you live."

" Praise th' Lord!" exclaimed Abe, "I knew
my Father would not see me want." So from that
time our old friend received his weekly allowance.

and was kept from want. The Lord takes care of His own children that trust in Him, and He often does so through the agency of some other individual, yet whomsoever he be, he shall have his reward. "Whosoever shall give to drink unto one of these little ones a cup of cold water only in the name of a disciple, verily I say unto you, he shall in no wise lose his reward " (Matt. x. 42).

OUT OF HARNESS.

When our old friend became so infirm as to be unable to work for his daily bread, we may naturally conclude that his labours as a local preacher also necessarily terminated. It was a great trouble to him to have to put off the harness; he struggled against it as long as he could, until indeed it was no longer safe for him to go to his beloved work; so he was compelled to stay at home, but never man left a calling with greater regret than he did this, for he loved it with all his heart.

Nor was he alone in his regrets. Many shared in them when it was known up and down that Little Abe was "out of harness," and would come no more. Some friends sitting together in one of the country places of the Circuit were talking about the preachers they had heard in that place, some of them in heaven, and some remaining till God should call them home; reference was made to Abe Lockwood, or as he was often called in the latter days of his life, "Old Abe!" "Ah, there's dear 'Old Abe!' he'll never come again." A fine little fellow that sat listening to the conversation rose to his feet, with his eyes full of tears, and exclaimed, "Why won't they let him come? If he only came and stood in the pulpit for us to see him, it would do." Old Abe was a great favourite with children, and he was always fond of them; sometimes old age turns folks sour, crabby, and snarlish with children, but age only mellowed him, and made him more loving and loved.

"WHERE'S 'T YOUNG PRAACHER?"

An amusing incident came under my notice during the time I was minister at Wellhouse in the Huddersfield Circuit. I was in the front garden one windy morning, attending to a few plants, and endeavouring to protect them against the gusty wind, when I thought I heard someone calling my name, but on looking up and seeing no one I resumed my task. In a moment or two I heard someone say, "Bless th' Lord! I've managed it at last, hurrah!" and on looking up, I saw Little Abe struggling along the steep pathway in a field just in front of my house, his head bare, his hat in his hand, his white locks tossed in wild confusion by the gale, yet holding on by their roots, refusing to part from their place of nativity.

"Well, I declare, here's Little Abe tipping about in the wind like a shuttlecock." Out I ran, and getting hold of his arm towed him into dock.

"Whatever has brought you here in such a gale of wind, Abe?"

"Hurrah! I'st see him naa," was his only response.

"See who?"

"Why, th' young praacher to be sure; ha'nt ye gotton a young praacher in your haase? I've come to see him." So laughing heartily at Abe's way of installing new members into the ministry, I opened the door and pushed him into the house. My wife was as much astonished at his arrival as I was, yet very glad to see him, especially when he inquired "Where's t'young praacher? Let's see him. Come, hold him up; there, naa, put him on my lap and let me have a bit of talk to him." And down he sat, and the "young praacher," at that time having advanced to the age of eight or ten weeks, was placed in the old man's lap, where he lay complacently winking his eye at Abe while he told him how he had left home after breakfast and walked over the hills about five miles in a storm of wind on purpose to make the acquaintance of this "young praacher" whose name was already on the Circuit plan. And there he stayed for the day, talking, singing, and communing with his young friend till evening, when we sent him home by the train.

Well, the time came when dear old Abe visited his friends nor stood in the familiar pulpits any more; then everyone, young and old, felt they

12

had sustained a loss. Yet this is the natural course of things all the world over; the scenes of life are continually changing, so are the most familiar and most beloved faces in those scenes; they come, and come, and come again, until we unconsciously acquire the habit of expecting them, but when at length they do not reappear as formerly, we realize an unexpected loss.

How many grand and familiar faces have disappeared from our pulpits and sanctuaries since we first began to remember things! In running the mind's eye back into byegone years, what a number we can call into recollection who are gone, never to return; while the truth is forced upon us, we are daily hurrying after them, and ere long some others will miss our faces from among the familiar scenes, and let us hope, will regret our absence.

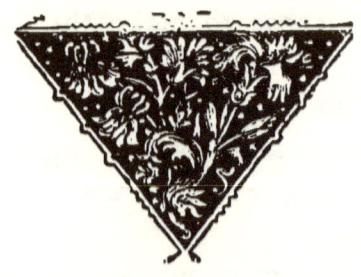

CHAPTER XXIII.

"Better is the End of a Thing than the Beginning."

IT was known by Little Abe that his infirmities were premonitory of the end which was not far off. He knew that though he might be permitted to linger for a while in the border land, he must soon receive command to march over the boundary, and enter the eternal world. Just as a shock of corn remains in the field to dry and ripen after the shearing, so our old friend remained in his place here for a short time, ripening for the heavenly garner.

He had just sufficient strength to go quietly about among his old friends in the village, and talk over the good things of his Father's kingdom; or he could get as far as the chapel, which was ever dear to him, and the more so now that he felt the time was fast approaching when he should enter it no more. He knew that before long his

happy spirit would be called up to worship in a
grander temple, among a multitude of those "who
had washed their robes, and made them white in
the blood of the Lamb;" and as he sat in old
Salem, and listened to the sweet notes of the
organ, his thoughts were oft carried away to the
great temple above, where day and night the
harpers are striking their joyous strings to the
Redeemer's praise.   Often when the choir chanted
those solemn words :—

"What shall I be, my Lord, when I behold Thee,
    In awful majesty at God's right hand ;
And 'mid th' eternal glories that enfold me,
    In strange bewilderment, O Lord, I stand ?
What shall I be ? these tears,—they dim my sight,
I cannot catch the blissful vision right,"

he was like one enraptured, as with tearful eyes,
quivering lips, and clasped hands he listened to
the soul-stirring hymn.   Little Abe was ripening
for the end.

"Arise! let us go up to Bethel."

A touching little incident is told of him about
this time. He always retained an affectionate
regard for the old tree on Almondbury Common,
where many years before he had made his peace
with God, and now a strong desire was felt by
him to visit the consecrated spot once more before
he died. It was his Bethel pillar; against that

old tree he had rested his weary head on the dark
night of his desolation; there the Lord God had
appeared to him, and filled his soul with the joys
of his salvation; there the morning of a new life
first broke upon his troubled spirit; there he had
made a covenant with the God of Jacob. That
old pillar was anointed with the first tears of
sanctified joy which ever fell from his eyes; it
was the altar on which he offered his broken and
renewed heart to God, and he felt as if the Lord
had given it to him as an inheritance and a monument of His pardoning mercy.

He must see it once more and renew his vows
to God; so one day they wrapped him up in his
great coat, and gave him his stick, and sent him
forth alone to his first sanctuary. Feebly and
slowly the old man made his way to the spot, and
standing on the very ground, and with his hand
upon the same old tree, he saw how the locality
was altered. Men had been busy during these
years, population had increased in the neighbourhood, houses were built in different places, and
many changes had taken place. But there still
remained the little running stream close by,—
figure to him of the stream of Divine grace, that
had never been cut off, never dried up in the
drought of summer, never stopped by the chill
of winter, never lost in the wild growth of the
wilderness world; but on and on it flowed, down
the incline of the moral world, winding and turning

from side to side, as if to gladden all in its course, away down the hill among the gaps of the rocks, and over the gravelly ground of human life, until it finds its way again into the river of God's eternal love. And there too, stood the tree, the monument ; but both man and tree bore unmistakable marks of age. The unwearying fingers of time had planted innumerable mosses against its bark ; some of its old branches had withered, its foliage was scantier than of old ; it was ripe, too; man and tree were both ripe and ready to fall.

What a sympathy there was between them, what a friendship, what a secret! How many storms had both those old trees encountered since God first threw them together! The old elm had shaken, bent, and groaned under the violent grasp of the tempest, which hundreds of times had swept across that common. But it still stood, patiently and bravely waiting, amid the rolling years, for the end. Brave old elm ! There is no sympathy in a tree, or this final meeting would have awakened it; but what matter ? There is enough in man for the tree and himself too, enough to kindle regard in his heart for every square inch of timber in that old trunk; enough to make him see eyes in every joint—loving eyes, looking at him in mute affection ; enough to transform every limb into strong arms stretched out to protect the old man in his feebleness, and enable him to see a smile in every wrinkling crack and fissure in thy hard, weather-beaten bark. Dear old elm, there needs no apology if a man love thee.

Who could wonder if Old Abe felt something like this for that tree? we should wonder if he did not. There, Old Abe, dear trembling old man, rest thy white, honoured head against the breast of that elm, and weep if thou wilt, and never mind whether man understand thee or not, God does. Weep, old man, but not in fear; thou hast nothing to fear, God is with thee, and " the place whereon thou standest is holy ground." It is the natural vent for those feelings which come crowding in upon thee, some from the long past, and some from the approaching future, now rapidly drawing on, with all its revelations of wonder and delight.

And thus old Abe stood with his head resting against the tree, his eyes closed, his tears running, and his lips silently moving in prayer to God; so he paid his vows once more, and gathered strength for the few remaining days of his pilgrimage; then he retraced his steps towards home, and by the time he arrived there he was entirely himself again, and no one would guess the emotion he had felt at Bethel.

" Well, Sally," he exclaimed, as he re-entered his cottage, "I've been to th' owd spot! They have hewn all abaat it, but th' owd tree stands yet. God 'll keep that tree while I live, and then they may do what they like wi' it."

So Abe went on, quietly severing himself from one tie after another which bound him to this world, and getting ready for his departure to another and a better.   His mind was now stead-fastly turned towards the future, and he was continually looking for his promised rest.   The nearer he got to the end of his life, the clearer his prospects of heaven became ; he enjoyed a most unclouded hope of glory.   Often he would say, when talking with his friends, " You'll be hearing some mornin' before lang that Abe is gone, and yo' needn't ask where.   Tak' my word for it, I'll be in glory.   If you should hear I'm dead, you may set it daan that I'm in heaven."

A brother local preacher had lain ill for some time, expecting every day to be his last.   Abe thought he would like to see him once more before he passed away, and accordingly he went, and the two old veterans spent a happy time together, conversing about the joys which were before them.   "We're both aat of harness naa, thaa sees," said Abe, "and we'll sooin be at haam.   I want the' to tell them I'm coming, and shall n't be long after the'."

Everyone thought that Abe would live the longer of the two, but he gained his prize first, passing away a little before his brother, and now they both "rest from their labours, and their works do follow them."

Abe's remaining strength rapidly failed him at

the last, so that he was unable to leave his room ;
yet he was always happy in prospect of the im-
mortal life before him. " No aching bones or
tottering limbs there," he would say; " Glory to
God ! I shall sooin be young agean." The Bible
and hymn-book were his constant companions now,
and in peaceful expectation he waited for the
signal that would open to him the portals of the
skies.

The annual lovefeast was held during the time
when he was a prisoner in his room, and it was a
privation to him not to be able to get there once
more, but it was not to be. They would hear his
voice no more in Salem, but before long he would
have to relate his enrapturing story among listening angels and saints before the throne. Several
of the friends came down from the chapel to see
him. He said, " Aye, lads, I could loike to ha' been
amang yo' once maar, but th' next toime I cross
Salem doorstep I shall be carried over ; but ne'er
moind, I have seen a door opened in heaven, and I
shall sooin go through—hallelujah ! "

At last he took to his bed never to rise again ;
the time of his departure was at hand. As, however,
his body lost strength, his spirit seemed to gain it ;
the words of the psalmist were ever on his lips,
" Though I walk through the valley of the shadow
of death, I will fear no evil, for Thou art with me,
Thy rod and Thy staff, they comfort me."

" Listen," he said one day, " when I can't spaike

to tell yo' haa I feel, I'll lift my hand, and yo'll knaw all's weal." This was for their sakes. He wanted to leave a token with his dear wife and children that should antidote their sorrow when he was gone.

A friend came one day from a distant town to see him; he felt very sad at finding him so near his end, and could not refrain from tears, but when the old man saw him weep, he began to repeat as well as his feeble voice would allow—

> " Break off your tears, ye saints, and tell
> How high your great Deliverer reigns ;
> See how He spoiled the hosts of hell,
> And led the monster Death in chains."

And then he took the part of comforter : " Aye, my lad, what art ta looking so sad abaat ? Thaa mun't be cast daan, thaa mun come up aat o' th' valley ; bless th' Lord !" he ran on, " I'm on Pisgah, and my soul is full of glory. I'm in soight o' th' promised land, hallelujah ! I'll sooin be at haam."

In this happy frame he continued to the last. As long as he could speak at all, words of exultation and praise rose to his lips, and when he could no longer articulate, he fell back upon the signal, and lifted his hand, in token that all was well. Dear old Abe, he was come to the end of his course, the shades of death were upon him, he was crossing the narrow strip of neutral ground that divides the two worlds ; friends stood in the margin of the shadow-land, watching him feebly lift his hand as he went over, till he could lift it no more, and when the signal dropt mourners knew that Old Abe was safe through.

He died in the Lord in November 1871, and left a memory behind that grows more fragrant as years go on. His dust lies buried in the graveyard in front of Salem Chapel, where, five years later, the remains of his devoted wife, Sally, were laid beside him. There let their dust sleep until that day "when they that are in their graves shall hear His voice, and come forth."

"Oh," said a good woman one day when talking over the subject of these pages, "I should just like to have an odd look into heaven, to see what Little Abe is about." What is he about? He is praising God in the glorious temple above : "And one of the elders answered, saying unto me, What are these arrayed in white robes ? and whence came they ? And I said unto him, Sir, thou knowest. And he said to me, These are they which came out of great tribulation, and have washed their robes, and made them white in the blood of the Lamb. Therefore are they before the throne of God, and serve Him day and night in the temple. They rest not day and night saying, Holy, Holy, Holy, Lord God Almighty, which was, and is, and is to come."

THE END.

Standard & Popular Works

PUBLISHED BY

T. WOOLMER, 2, CASTLE STREET, CITY ROAD, E.C.

PRICE SIX SHILLINGS.

The Light of the World : Lessons from the Life of Our Lord for Children. By the Rev. RICHARD NEWTON, DD., Author of *Rays from the Sun of Righteousness*, etc., etc., etc. Fcap. 4to. Numerous Illusts.
'A most attractive and deeply interesting Sunday book for children.'

PRICE FIVE SHILLINGS.

Sermons by the Rev. W. MORLEY PUNSHON, LL.D. With a Preface by the Rev. W. ARTHUR, M.A. These Sermons contain the latest Corrections of the Author. Two Volumes. Crown 8vo. 5/- each.
'Here we have found, in rare combination, pure and elevated diction, conscience-searching appeal, withering exposure of sin, fearless advocacy of duty, forceful putting of truth,' etc., etc.—*London Quarterly Review.*

Lectures by the Rev. W. MORLEY PUNSHON, LL.D. Crown 8vo.
'One and all of the Lectures are couched in the powerful and popular style which distinguished the great preacher, and they are worthy of a permanent place in any library.'—*Daily Chronicle.*

Toward the Sunrise : being Sketches of Travel in Europe and the East. To which is added a Memorial Sketch (with Portrait) of the Rev. W. MORLEY PUNSHON, LL.D. By HUGH JOHNSTON, M.A., B.D. Crown 8vo. Numerous Illustrations.

Fiji and the Fijians ; and Missionary Labours among the Cannibals. Sixth Thousand. Revised and Supplemented with Index. By Rev. JAMES CALVERT ; and a Preface by C. F. GORDON CUMMING, Author of *At Home in Fiji*, etc. Crown 8vo, with Portrait of Thakombau, a Map, and numerous Illustrations.

PRICE FOUR SHILLINGS.

Our Indian Empire : its Rise and Growth. By the Rev. J. SHAW BANKS. Imperial 16mo. Thirty-five Illustrations and Map.
'The imagination of the young will be fired by its stirring stories of English victories, and it will do much to make history popular.'—*Daily Chronicle.*
'A well condensed and sensibly written popular narrative of Anglo-Indian History.'—*Daily News.*

Zoology of the Bible. By HARLAND COULTAS. Preface by the Rev. W. F. MOULTON, D.D. Imperial 16mo. 126 Illustrations.
'We have in a most convenient form all that is worth knowing of the discoveries of modern science which have any reference to the animals mentioned in Scripture.'—*Preacher's Budget.*

Missionary Anecdotes, Sketches, Facts, and Incidents. By the Rev. WILLIAM MOISTER. Imperial 16mo. Eight Page Illustrations.
'The narratives are many of them very charming.'—*Sword and Trowel*

12-84.

Northern Lights; or, Pen and Pencil Sketches of Nineteen
Modern Scottish Worthies. By the Rev. J. MARRAT. Crown 8vo. Portraits
and Illustrations.
'It is a charming book in every sense.'—*Irish Evangelist.*

The Brotherhood of Men ; or, Christian Sociology. By Rev.
W. UNSWORTH.

PRICE THREE SHILLINGS AND SIXPENCE.

Sabbath Chimes : A Meditation in Verse for the Sundays of a
Year. By Dr. PUNSHON. Crown 8vo, gilt edges.

Uncle Jonathan's Walks in and Around London. Foolscap
4to. Profusely Illustrated.

Our Sea-Girt Isle : English Scenes and Scenery Delineated.
By the Rev. J. MARRAT. Imperial 16mo. Map and 153 Illustrations.
'An unusually readable and attractive book.'—*Christian World.*

Rambles in Bible Lands By the Rev. RICHARD NEWTON,
D.D. Imperial 16mo. Seventy Illustrations.
'From the juvenile stand-point, we can speak in hearty commendation of
it.'—*Literary World.*

'Land of the Mountain and the Flood' : Scottish Scenes
and Scenery Delineated. By the Rev. JABEZ MARRAT. Imperial 16mo.
Map and Seventy-six Illustrations.
'Described with taste, judgment, and accuracy of detail.'—*Scotsman.*

Popery and Patronage. Biographical Illustrations of Scotch
Church History. By the Rev. J. MARRAT. Imperial 16mo. Ten Illustrations.
'Most instructive biographical narratives.'—*Derbyshire Courier.*

Wycliffe to Wesley : Heroes and Martyrs of the Church in
Britain. Imperial 16mo. Twenty-four Portraits and Forty other Illustrations.
'We give a hearty welcome to this handsomely got up and interesting
volume.'—*Literary World.*

John Lyon ; or, From the Depths. By RUTH ELLIOTT.
Crown 8vo. Five Full-page Illustrations.
'Earnest and eloquent, dramatic in treatment, and thoroughly healthy in
spirit.'—*Birmingham Daily Gazette.*

The Thorough Business Man : Memoir of Walter Powell,
Merchant. By Rev. B. GREGORY. Seventh Edition. Crn. 8vo, with Portrait.

The Life of Gideon Ouseley. By the Rev. WILLIAM
ARTHUR, M.A. Eighth Thousand. Crown 8vo, with Portrait.

The Aggressive Character of Christianity. By Rev. W.
UNSWORTH.

Garton Rowley ; or, Leaves from the Log of a Master
Mariner. By J. JACKSON WRAY. Crown 8vo.

Honest John Stallibrass. By J. JACKSON WRAY. Crown 8vo.

A Man Every Inch of Him. By J. JACKSON WRAY. Crn. 8vo.

Paul Meggitt's Delusion. By J. JACKSON WRAY. Crown 8vo.

Nestleton Magna. A Story of Yorkshire Methodism. By J.
JACKSON WRAY. Crown 8vo.

Chronicles of Capstan Cabin ; or, the Children's Hour. By
J. JACKSON WRAY. Imperial 16mo. Twenty-eight Illustrations.

Missionary Stories, Narratives, Scenes, and Incidents. By the Rev. W. MOISTER. Crown 8vo. Eight Page Illustrations.
' Intensely interesting.' —*Methodist New Connexion Magazine.*

Scenes and Adventures in Great Namaqualand. By the Rev. B. RIDSDALE. Crown 8vo, with Portrait.

Melissa's Victory. By ASHTON NEILL. Crown 8vo, gilt edges. Illustrations by GUNSTON.

Two Saxon Maidens. By ELIZA KERR. Crown 8vo, gilt edges. Illustrations by GUNSTON.

Gems Reset; or, the Wesleyan Catechisms Illustrated by Imagery and Narrative. Crown 8vo. By Rev. B. SMITH.

Vice-Royalty; or, a Royal Domain held for the King, and enriched by the King. Crown 8vo. Twelve page Illustns. By Rev. B. SMITH.

Sunshine in the Kitchen; or, Chapters for Maid Servants. Fourth Thousand. Crown 8vo. Numerous Illustrations. By Rev. B. SMITH.

Way-Marks : Placed by Royal Authority on the King's Highway. Being One Hundred Scripture Proverbs, Enforced and Illustrated. Crown 8vo. Eight Page Engravings. By Rev. B. SMITH.

The Great Army of London Poor. Sketches of Life and Character in a Thames-side District. By the River-side Visitor. Third Edition. Crown 8vo. 540 pp. Eight Illustrations.
' Admirably told. The author has clearly lived and mingled with the people he writes about.'—*Guardian.*

PRICE TWO SHILLINGS AND SIXPENCE.

Elias Power, of Ease-in-Zion. By Rev. JOHN M. BAMFORD. Fourth Thousand. Crown 8vo. Seventeen Illustrations. Gilt edges.

Life of John Wicklif. By Rev. W. L. WATKINSON. Portrait and Eleven Illustrations. Crown 8vo.

Good News for Children; or, God's Love to the Little Ones. By JOHN COLWELL. Crown 8vo, gilt edges. Fourteen Illustrations.

Pleasant Talks about Jesus. By JOHN COLWELL. Crown 8vo.

Little Abe ; or, the Bishop of Berry Brow. Being the Life of Abraham Lockwood, a quaint and popular Local Preacher. By F. JEWELL. Crown 8vo, gilt edges. With Portrait.
' The racy, earnest, vernacular speech of *Little Abe,* and his quaint illustrations and home-thrusts, are humorous indeed. . . . Cannot fail to be a favourite.'—*Christian Age.*

Cecily : a Tale of the English Reformation. By EMMA LESLIE. Crown 8vo. Five full-page Illustrations.
' This is an interesting and attractive little book. . . . It is lively and healthy in tone.'—*Literary World.*

Glimpses of India and Mission Life. By Mrs. HUTCHEON Crown 8vo. Eight Page Illustrations.
' A well-written account of Indian life in its social aspects, by the wife of an Indian missionary.'—*British Quarterly.*

The Beloved Prince : a Memoir of His Royal Highness, the Prince Consort. By WILLIAM NICHOLS. Crown 8vo. With Portrait and Nineteen Illustrations. Cloth, gilt edges.
' An admirable condensation of a noble life.'—*Derbyshire Courier.*

Glenwood: a Story of School Life. By JULIA K. BLOOM-
FIELD. Crown 8vo. Seven Illustrations.

> 'A useful book for school-girls who think more of beauty and dress than of brains and grace.'—*Sword and Trowel.*

Undeceived: Roman or Anglican? A Story of English
Ritualism. By RUTH ELLIOTT. Crown 8vo.

> 'In the creation and description of character the work belongs to the highest class of imaginative art.'—*Free Church of England Magazine.*

Self-Culture and Self-Reliance, under God the Means of
Self-Elevation. By the Rev. W. UNSWORTH. Crown 8vo.

> 'An earnest, thoughtful, eloquent book on an important subject.'—*Folkestone News.*

A Pledge that Redeemed Itself. By SARSON, Author of
' Blind Olive,' etc. Crown 8vo. Numerous Illustrations. Gilt edges.

> 'We are informed in the preface that it is " an etching from life," and we can well believe it, for it bears all the marks of a genuine study of living men and women.'—*Literary World.*

Old Daniel; or, Memoirs of a Converted Hindu. By the Rev.
T. HODSON. Crown 8vo, gilt edges. Coloured Illustrations.

The Story of a Peninsular Veteran: Sergeant in the 43rd
Light Infantry during the Peninsular War. Crown 8vo. 13 Illustrations.

> 'Full of adventure, told in a religious spirit. We recommend this narrative to boys and young men.'—*Hastings and St. Leonard's News.*

Rays from the Sun of Righteousness. By the Rev. RICHARD
NEWTON, D.D. Crown 8vo. Eleven Illustrations. Gilt edges.

In the Tropics; or, Scenes and Incidents of West Indian Life.
By the Rev. JABEZ MARRAT. Crown 8vo, gilt edges, Illustrations, etc.

> 'A vivid description of scenes and incidents, . . . with an interesting record of the progress of mission work.'—*Sheffield Post.*

Climbing: a Manual for the Young who Desire to Rise in
Both Worlds. By the Rev. BENJAMIN SMITH. Crown 8vo. Sixth Edition.

Our Visit to Rome, with Notes by the Way. By the
Rev. JOHN RHODES. Royal 16mo. Forty-five Illustrations.

The Lancasters and their Friends. A Tale of Methodist
Life. By S. J. F. Crown 8vo.

Those Boys. By FAYE HUNTINGTON. Crown 8vo. Illustrated.

Leaves from my Log of Twenty-five years' Christian
Work in the Port of London. Crown 8vo. Eight Illustrations.

East End Pictures; or, More Leaves from My Log
of Twenty-five Years' Christian Work. By T. C. GARLAND. Crown 8vo. Portrait and Five Illustrations.

The Willow Pattern: A Story Illustrative of Chinese Social
Life. By the Rev. HILDERIC FRIEND. Crown 8vo, gilt edges. Numerous Illustrations.

Passages from the Diary of an Early Methodist. By
RICHARD ROWE.

Orphans of the Forest; or, His Little Jonathan. By A. E.
COURTENAY. Foolscap 8vo. Four Illustrations.

MARK GUY PEARSE'S WORKS.

Nine Volumes, Crown 8vo, Cloth, Gilt Edges. Price 2s. 6d. each.

1.—Daniel Quorm, and his Religious Notions. FIRST SERIES. 70,000.

2.—Daniel Quorm, and his Religious Notions. SECOND SERIES. 22,000.

3.—Sermons for Children. 19,000.

4.—Mister Horn and his Friends; or, Givers and Giving. 21,000.

5.—Short Stories, and other Papers. 8000.

6.—'Good Will': a Collection of Christmas Stories. 9000.

7.—Simon Jasper. 11,000.

8.—Cornish Stories. 6000.

9.—Homely Talks. 11,000.

'Scarcely any living writer can construct a parable better, more quaintly, simply, and congruously. His stories are equally clever and telling. . . . One secret of their spell is that they are brimful of heart. . . . His books should be in every school library.'—*British Quarterly Review.*

Thoughts on Holiness. By MARK GUY PEARSE. Eleventh Thousand. Royal 16mo. Cloth, red edges.

PRICE TWO SHILLINGS.

Punchi Nona : A Story of Female Education and Village Life in Ceylon. By the Rev. SAMUEL LANGDON. Crown 8vo. Numerous Illustrations.

Friends and Neighbours: A Story for Young Children. Crown 8vo. Illustrated.

The Oakhurst Chronicles : A Tale of the Times of Wesley. By ANNIE E. KEELING. Crown 8vo. Four Illustrations.
'This beautiful story.'—*Sheffield Independent.*
'A fascinating story.'—*Christian Age.*

Poet Toilers in Many Fields. By Mrs. R. A. WATSON. Crown 8vo. Thirteen Illustrations.

The 'Good Luck' of the Maitlands: a Family Chronicle. By Mrs. R. A. WATSON. Five Illustrations. Crown 8vo.

Valeria, the Martyr of the Catacombs. A Tale of Early Christian Life in Rome. By the Rev. W. H. WITHROW, D.D. Crown 8vo. Illustrations.

Tina and Beth; or, the Night Pilgrims. By ANNIE E. COURTENAY. Crown 8vo. Frontispiece.

Wilfred Hedley ; or, How Teetotalism Came to Ellensmere. By S. J. FITZGERALD. Crown 8vo. Frontispiece.

Equally Yoked: and other Stories. By S. J. FITZGERALD. Frontispiece.

Master and Man. By S. J. FITZGERALD. Frontispiece.

Coals and Colliers ; or, How we Get the Fuel for our Fires. By S. J. FITZGERALD. Crown 8vo. Illustrations.
'An interesting description of how we get the fuel for our fires, illustrated by tales of miners' families.'—*Christian World.*

James Daryll; or, From Honest Doubt to Christian Faith.
By RUTH ELLIOTT. Crown 8vo.
'We have seldom read a more beautiful story than this.'—*The Echo.*

The King's Messenger: a Story of Canadian Life. By the
Rev. W. H. WITHROW, M.A. Crown 8vo.

Illustrations of Fulfilled Prophecy. By the Rev. J. ROBINSON
GREGORY. Crown 8vo. Numerous Illustrations.

The Basket of Flowers. Illustrated. Crown 8vo, gilt edges.

The Great Apostle; or, Pictures from the Life of St. Paul.
By the Rev. JABEZ MARRAT. Foolscap 8vo. 28 Illustrations and Map.
'A charming little book. . . . Written in a style that must commend itself
to young people.'—*Sunday-School Times.*

Martin Luther, the Prophet of Germany. By the Rev. J.
SHAW BANKS. Foolscap 8vo. 13 Illustrations.
'Mr. Banks has succeeded in packing a great deal of matter into a small
space, and yet has told his story in a very attractive style.'—*London
Quarterly Review.*

Sir Walter Raleigh: Pioneer of Anglo-American Colonisation.
By CHARLES K. TRUE, D.D. Foolscap 8vo. 16 Illustrations.
'We have here a book which we strongly recommend to our young readers.
It will do boys good to read it.'—*The Methodist.*

Homes and Home Life in Bible Lands. By J. R. S.
CLIFFORD. Foolscap 8vo. Eighty Illustrations.
'A useful little volume respecting the manners and customs of Eastern
nations. It brings together, in a small compass, much that will be of service
to the young student of the Bible.'—*Watchman.*

Hid Treasures, and the Search for Them: Lectures to
Bible Classes. By the Rev. J. HARTLEY. Foolscap 8vo. With Frontispiece.

Youthful Obligations. Illustrated by a large number of Appropriate Facts and Anecdotes. Foolscap 8vo With Illustrations.

Eminent Christian Philanthropists: Brief Biographical
Sketches, designed especially as Studies for the Young. By the Rev.
GEORGE MAUNDER. Fcap. 8vo. Nine Illustrations.

The Tower, the Temple, and the Minster: Historical and
Biographical Associations of the Tower of London, St. Paul's Cathedral,
and Westminster Abbey. By the Rev. J. W. THOMAS. Second Edition.
Foolscap 8vo. 14 Illustrations.

Peter Pengelly; or, 'True as the Clock.' By J. J. WRAY.
Crown 8vo. Forty Illustrations.
'A famous book for boys.'—*The Christian.*

The Stolen Children. By Rev. H. BLEBY. Foolscap 8vo.
Six Illustrations.

My Coloured Schoolmaster: and other Stories. By the Rev.
H. BLEBY. Foolscap 8vo. Five Illustrations.
'The narratives are given in a lively, pleasant manner that is well suited to
gain and keep alive the attention of juvenile readers.'—*The Friend.*

Female Heroism and Tales of the Western World. By
the Rev. H. BLEBY. Foolscap 8vo. Four Illustrations.

Capture of the Pirates: with other Stories of the Western Seas.
By the Rev. HENRY BLEBY. Foolscap 8vo. Four Illustrations.
'The stories are graphically told, and will inform on some phases of
Western life.'—*Warrington Guardian.*

The Prisoner's Friend : The Life of Mr. JAMES BUNDY, of
Bristol. By his Grandson, the Rev. W. R. WILLIAMS. Foolscap 8vo.

Kilkee. By ELIZA KERR, author of *Slieve Bloom.*

Adelaide's Treasure, and How the Thief came Unawares.
By SARSON, Author of 'A Pledge that Redeemed Itself,' etc. Four Illustrations.
'This graphic story forms an episode in the history of Wesleyan Missions
in Newfoundland.'—*Christian Age.*

Two Snowy Christmas Eves. By ELIZA KERR. Royal
16mo. Gilt edges. Six Illustrations.

PRICE EIGHTEENPENCE.

'Little Ray' Series. Royal 16mo.

Little Ray and her Friends. By RUTH ELLIOTT. Five
Illustrations.

The Breakfast Half-Hour : Addresses on Religious and Moral
Topics. By the Rev. H. R. BURTON. Twenty-five Illustrations.
'Practical, earnest, and forcible.'—*Literary World.*

Gleanings in Natural History for Young People. Profusely
Illustrated.

Broken Purposes ; or, the Good Time Coming. By LILLIE
MONTFORT. Five Page Illustrations. Gilt edges.

The History of the Tea-Cup : with a Descriptive Account of
the Potter's Art. By the Rev. G. R. WEDGWOOD. Profusely Illustrated.

The Cliftons and their Play-Hours. By Mrs. COSSLETT.
Seven Page Illustrations.

The Lilyvale Club and its Doings. By EDWIN A. JOHNSON,
D.D. Seven Page Illustrations.
'The "doings" of the club decidedly deserve a careful perusal.'—
Literary World.

The Bears' Den. By E. H. MILLER. Six Page Illustrations.
'A capital story for boys.'—*Christian Age.*

Ned's Motto ; or, Little by Little. By the author of 'Faithful
and True,' 'Tony Starr's Legacy.' Six Page Illustrations.
'The story of a boy's struggles to do right, and his influence over other
boys. The book is well and forcibly written.'—*The Christian.*

A Year at Riverside Farm. By E. H. MILLER. Royal 16mo.
Six Page Illustrations.
'A book of more than common interest and power.'—*Christian Age.*

The Royal Road to Riches. By E. H. MILLER. Fifteen
Illustrations.

Maude Linden ; or, Working for Jesus. By LILLIE MONTFORT.
Four Illustrations.
'Intended to enforce the value of personal religion, especially in Christian
work. . . . Brightly and thoughtfully written.'—*Liverpool Daily Post.*

Oscar's Boyhood ; or, the Sailor's Son. By DANIEL WISE,
D.D. Six Illustrations.
'A healthy story for boys, written in a fresh and vigorous style, and
plainly teaching many important lessons.'—*Christian Miscellany.*

Summer Days at Kirkwood. By E. H. MILLER. Four
Illustrations.

'Capital story; conveying lessons of the highest moral import.'—*Sheffield Post.*

Slieve Bloom. By ELIZA KERR, Author of *The Golden City.*
Three Illustrations.

'The style of the book is graphic, and of considerable literary merit.'—*Literary World.*

'A real children's story, well told, with many beautiful touches of an artist's hand, and the evidences of a true woman's heart.'—*Christian Age.*

Holy-days and Holidays; or, Memories of the Calendar for
Young People. By J. R. S. CLIFFORD. Numerous Illustrations.

'Instruction and amusement are blended in this little volume.—*The Christian.*

Talks with the Bairns about Bairns. By RUTH ELLIOTT.
Illustrated.

'Pleasantly written, bright, and in all respects attractive.'—*Leeds Mercury.*

My First Class : and other Stories. By RUTH ELLIOTT.
Illustrated.

'The stories are full of interest, well printed, nicely illustrated, and tastefully bound. It is a volume which will be a favourite in any family of children.'—*Derbyshire Courier.*

Luther Miller's Ambition. By LILLIE MONTFORT. Gilt
edges. Illustrated by GUNSTON.

'*Wee Donald' Series.*' Royal 16mo.

An Old Sailor's Yarn : and other Sketches from Daily Life.

The Stony Road : a Tale of Humble Life.

Stories for Willing Ears. For Boys. By T. S. E.

Stories for Willing Ears. For Girls. By T. S. E.

Thirty Thousand Pounds : and other Sketches from Daily Life.

'Wee Donald' : Sequel to 'Stony Road.'

PRICE EIGHTEENPENCE. *Foolscap 8vo Series.*

Two Standard Bearers in the East : Sketches of Dr. DUFF
and Dr. Wuson. By Rev. J. MARRAT. Eight Illustrations.

Three Indian Heroes: the Missionary; the Soldier; the
Statesman. By the Rev. J. SHAW BANKS. Numerous Illustrations.

David Livingstone, Missionary and Discoverer. By the
Rev. J. MARRAT. Fifteen Page Illustrations.

'The story is told in a way which is likely to interest young people, and to quicken their sympathy with missionary work.'—*Literary World.*

Columbus; or, the Discovery of America. By GEORGE
CUFITT. Seventeen Illustrations.

Cortes; or, the Discovery and Conquest of Mexico. By
GEORGE CUBITT. Nine Illustrations.

Pizarro; or, the Discovery and Conquest of Peru. By GEORGE
CUBITT. Nine Illustrations.

Granada; or, the Expulsion of the Moors from Spain. By
GEORGE CUBITT. Seven Illustrations.

James Montgomery, Christian Poet and Philanthropist.
By the Rev. J. MARRAT. Eleven Illustrations.
'The book is a welcome and tasteful addition to our biographical knowledge.'—*Warrington Guardian.*

The Father of Methodism : the Life and Labours of the Rev.
John Wesley, A.M. By Mrs. COSSLETT. Forty-five Illustrations.
'Presents a clear outline of the life of the founder of Methodism, and is calculated to create a desire for larger works upon the subject. The illustrations are numerous and effective.—quite a pictorial history in themselves.'

Old Truths in New Lights : Illustrations of Scripture Truth
for the Young. By W. H. S. Illustrated.

Chequer Alley : a Story of Successful Christian Work. By
the Rev. F. W. BRIGGS, M.A.

The Englishman's Bible : How he Got it, and Why he Keeps
it. By the Rev. JOHN BOVES, M.A. Thirteen Illustrations.

Home : and the Way to Make Home Happy. By the Rev.
DAVID HAY. With Frontispiece.

Helen Leslie ; or, Truth and Error. By ADELINE. Frontispiece.

Building her House. By Mrs. R. A. WATSON. Five Illustns.
'A charmingly written tale, illustrative of the power of Christian meekness.'
—*Christian World.*

Crabtree Fold : a Tale of the Lancashire Moors. By Mrs. R.
A. WATSON. Five Illustrations.

Davy's Friend : and other Stories. By JENNIE PERRETT.
'Excellent, attractive, and instructive.'—*The Christian.*

Arthur Hunter's First Shilling. By Mrs. CROWE.

Hill Side Farm. By ANNA J. BUCKLAND.

The Boy who Wondered ; or, Jack and Minnchen. By Mrs.
GEORGE GLADSTONE

Kitty ; or, The Wonderful Love. By A. E. COURTENAY.
Illustrated.

The River Singers. By W. ROBSON.

PRICE EIGHTEENPENCE. *Crown 8vo Series.*

Patty Thorne's Adventures. By Mrs. H. B. PAULL. Illustrated.

Fighting to Victory. By EZEKIEL ROGERS. Second Edition.

The Dairyman's Daughter. By the Rev. LEGH RICHMOND,
M.A. A New Edition, with Additions, giving an Authentic Account of her
Conversion, and of her connection with the Wesleyan Methodists.

Footsteps in the Snow. By ANNIE E. COURTENAY, Author
of *Tina and Beth*, etc., etc. Illustrated.
'Every page is genial, warm, and bright.'—*Irish Christian Advocate.*

The Beloved Prince : A Memoir of His Royal Highness
the Prince Con·ort. By WILLIAM NICHOLS. Nineteen Illustrations.

Drierstock : A Tale of Mission Work on the American Frontier.
Three Illustrations.

Go Work: A Book for Girls. By ANNIE FRANCES PERRAM.

Picture Truths. Practical Lessons on the Formation of Character, from Bible Emblems and Proverbs. By JOHN TAYLOR. Thirty Illustrations.

Those Watchful Eyes; or, Jemmy and his Friends. By EMILIE SEARCHFIELD. Frontispiece.

The Basket of Flowers. Four Illustrations.

Auriel, and other Stories. By RUTH ELLIOTT. Frontispiece.

A Voice from the Sea; or, The Wreck of the Eglantine. By RUTH ELLIOTT.

Rays from the Sun of Righteousness. By the Rev. R. NEWTON. Eleven Illustrations.

A Pledge that Redeemed Itself. By SARSON.
'A clever, sparkling, delightful story.'—*Sheffield Independent.*

In the Tropics; or, Scenes and Incidents of West Indian Life. By the Rev. J. MARRAT. Illustrations and Map.

Old Daniel; or, Memoirs of a Converted Hindu. By Rev. T. HODSON. Twelve Illustrations.

Little Abe; or, The Bishop of Berry Brow. Being the Life of Abraham Lockwood.

CHEAP EDITION OF MARK GUY PEARSE'S BOOKS.

Foolscap 8vo. Price Eighteenpence each.

1. Daniel Quorm, and his Religious Notions. 1ST SERIES.
2. Daniel Quorm, and his Religious Notions. 2ND SERIES.
3. Sermons for Children.
4. Mister Horn and his Friends; or, Givers and Giving.
5. Short Stories: and other Papers.
6. 'Good Will': a Collection of Christmas Stories.

PRICE ONE SHILLING. *Imperial 32mo. Cloth, gilt lettered.*

Abbott's Histories for the Young.
Vol. 1. Alexander the Great. Vol. 2. Alfred the Great. Vol. 3. Julius Cæsar.

PRICE ONE SHILLING. *Royal 16mo. Cloth, gilt lettered.*

Ancient Egypt: Its Monuments, Worship, and People. By the Rev. EDWARD LIGHTWOOD. Twenty-six Illustrations.

Vignettes from English History. From the Norman Conqueror to Henry IV. Twenty-three Illustrations.

Margery's Christmas Box. By RUTH ELLIOTT. Seven Illusts.

No Gains without Pains: a True Life for the Boys. By H. C. KNIGHT. Six Illustrations.

Peeps into the Far North: Chapters on Iceland, Lapland, and Greenland. By S. E. SCHOLES. Twenty-four Illustrations.

Lessons from Noble Lives, and other Stories. 31 Illustrations.

Stories of Love and Duty. For Boys and Girls. 31 Illusts.

The Railway Pioneers; or, the Story of the Stephensons, Father and Son. By H.C. KNIGHT. Fifteen Illustrations.

The Royal Disciple: Louisa, Queen of Prussia. By C.R. HURST. Six Illustrations.

Tiny Tim: a Story of London Life. Founded on Fact. By F. HORNER. Twenty-two Illustrations.

John Tregenoweth. His Mark. By MARK GUY PEARSE. Twenty-five Illustrations.

'I 'll Try'; or, How the Farmer's Son became a Captain. Ten Illustrations.

The Giants, and How to Fight Them. By Dr. RICHARD NEWTON. Fifteen Illustrations.

The Meadow Daisy. By LILLIE MONTFORT. Numerous Illustrations.

Robert Dawson; or, the Brave Spirit. Four Page Illustrations.

The Tarnside Evangel. By M. A. H. Eight Illustrations.

Rob Rat: a Story of Barge Life. By MARK GUY PEARSE. Numerous Illustrations.

The Unwelcome Baby, with other Stories of Noble Lives early Consecrated. By S. ELLEN GREGORY. Nine Illustrations.

Jane Hudson, the American Girl. Four Page Illustrations.

The Babes in the Basket; or, Daph and her Charge. Four Page Illustrations.

Insect Lights and Sounds. By J. R. S. CLIFFORD. Illustrns. 'A valuable little book for children, pleasantly illustrated.'—*The Friend.*

The Jew and his Tenants. By A. D. WALKER. Illustrated. 'A pleasant little story of the results of genuine Christian influence.'— *Christian Age.*

The History of Joseph: for the Young. By the Rev. T. CHAMPNESS. Twelve Illustrations. 'Good, interesting, and profitable.'—*Wesleyan Methodist Magazine.*

The Old Miller and his Mill. By MARK GUY PEARSE. Twelve Illustrations.

The First Year of my Life: a True Story for Young People. By ROSE CATHAY FRIEND. 'It is a most fascinating story.'—*Sunday School Times.*

Fiji and the Friendly Isles: Sketches of their Scenery and People. By S. E. SCHOLES. Fifteen Illustrations. 'We warmly recommend this little volume to readers of every sort.'— *Hastings and St. Leonard's News.*

The Story of a Pillow. Told for Children. Four Illustrations. 'Simply and gracefully told.'—*Bradford Observer.* 'Little folks are sure to be interested in this wonderful pillow.'—*Literary World.*

UNCLE DICK'S LIBRARY OF SHILLING BOOKS.

Foolscap 8vo. 128 pp. Cloth.

Uncle Dick's Legacy. By E. H. MILLER, Author of ' Royal Road to Riches,' etc., etc. Illustrated.
'A first-rate story . . . full of fun and adventure, but thoroughly good and healthy.'—*Christian Miscellany.*

Beatrice and Brian. By HELEN BRISTON. Three Illustrns.
'A very prettily told story about a wayward little lady and a large mastiff dog, specially adapted for girls.'—*Derbyshire Advertiser.*

Becky and Reubie; or, the Little Street Singers. By MINA E. GOULDING. Three Illustrations.
'A clever, pleasing, well-written story.'—*Leeds Mercury.*

Gilbert Guestling; or, the Story of a Hymn Book. Illustrated.
'It is a charmingly told story '—*Nottingham Daily Express.*

Guy Sylvester's Golden Year. Three Illustrations.
'A very pleasantly written story.'—*Derbyshire Courier.*

Left to Take Care of Themselves. By A. RYLANDS. Three Illustrations.

Tom Fletcher's Fortunes. By Mrs. H. B. PAULL. Three Illustrations.
'A capital book for boys.'—*Sheffield and Rotherham Independent.*

The Young Bankrupt, and other Stories. By Rev. JOHN COLWELL. Three Illustrations.

The Basket of Flowers. Four Illustrations.

Mattie and Bessie; or, Climbing the Hill. By A. E. COURTENAY.

Tom: A Woman's Work for Christ. By Rev. J. W. KEYWORTH. Six Illustrations.

The Little Disciple: The Story of his Life Told for Young Children. Six Illustrations.

Afterwards. By EMILIE SEARCHFIELD. Three Page Illustns.

Mischievous Foxes; or, the Little Sins that mar the Christian Character. By JOHN OLWELL. Price 1s.
'An amazing amount of sensible talk and sound advice.'—*The Christian.*

Joel Bulu: The Autobiography of a Native Minister in the South Seas. New Edition, with an account of his Last Days. Edited by the Rev. G. S. ROWE. Foolscap 8vo, cloth. Price 1s.

Robert Moffat, the African Missionary. By Rev. J. MARRAT. Foolscap 8vo, Illustrated. Price 1s.

The Dairyman's Daughter. By the Rev. LEGH RICHMOND, M.A. A New Edition, with Additions giving an Authentic Account of her Conversion, and of her connection with the Wesleyan Methodists.

Polished Stones from a Rough Quarry. By Mrs. HUTCHEON. Price 1s.
'A Scotch story of touching and pathetic interest. It illustrates the power of Christian sympathy '—*Irish Evangelist.*

Recollections of Methodist Worthies. Fcap 8vo. Price 1s.
'Deserves to be perused by members of all Christian communities.'—*Sword and Trowel.*

PRICE NINEPENCE. *Imperial 32mo. Cloth, Illuminated.*

1. The Wonderful Lamp : and other Stories. By RUTH ELLIOTT. Five Illustrations.
2. Dick's Troubles : and How He Met Them. By RUTH ELLIOTT. Six Illustrations.
3. The Chat in the Meadow : and other Stories. By LILLIE MONTFORT. Six Illustrations.
4. John's Teachers : and other Stories. By LILLIE MONT-FORT. Six Illustrations.
5. Nora Grayson's Dream : and other Stories. By LILLIE MONTFORT. Seven Illustrations.
6. Rosa's Christmas Invitations : and other Stories. By LILLIE MONTFORT. Six Illustrations.
7. Ragged Jim's Last Song : and other Ballads. By EDWARD BAILEY. Eight Illustrations.
8. Pictures from Memory. By ADELINE. Nine Illustrations.
9. The Story of the Wreck of the 'Maria' Mail Boat: with a Memoir of Mrs. Hincksman, the only Survivor. Illustrated.
10. Passages from the Life of Heinrich Stilling. Five Page Illustrations.
11. Little and Wise : The Ants, The Conies, The Locusts, and the Spiders. Twelve Illustrations.
12. Spoiling the Vines, and Fortune Telling. Eight Illusts.
13. The Kingly Breaker, Concerning Play, and Sowing the Seed.
14. The Fatherly Guide, Rhoda, and Fire in the Soul.
15. Short Sermons for Little People. By the Rev. T. CHAMPNESS.
16. Sketches from my Schoolroom. Four Illustrations.
17. Mary Ashton : A True Story of Eighty Years Ago. 4 Illusts.
18. The Little Prisoner : or, the Story of the Dauphin of France. Five Illustrations.
19. The Story of an Apprenticeship. By the Rev. A. LANGLEY. Frontispiece.
20. Mona Bell : or, Faithful in Little Things. By EDITH M. EDWARDS. Four Illustrations.
21. Minnie Neilson's Summer Holidays, and What Came of Them. By M. CAMBWELL. Four Illustrations.
22. After Many Days ; or, The Turning Point in James Power's Life. Three Illustrations.
23. Alfred May. By R. RYLANDS. Two coloured Illustrations.
24. Dots and Gwinnie : a Story of Two Friendships. By R. RYLANDS. Three Illustrations.
25. Little Sally. By MINA E. GOULDING. Six Illustrations.
26. Joe Webster's Mistake. By EMILIE SEARCHFIELD. Three Illustrations.
27. Muriel ; or, The Sister Mother.
28. Nature's Whispers.
29. Johnny's Work and How he did it. Five Illustrations.
30. Pages from a Little Girl's Life. By A. F. PERRAM. Five Illustrations.
31. The Wrens' Nest at Wrenthorpe. By A. E. KEELING. Five Illustrations.

PRICE EIGHTPENCE. *Imperial 32mo. Cloth, gilt edges.*

The whole of the Ninepenny Series are also sold in Limp Cloth at Eightpence.

Ancass, the Slave Preacher. By the Rev. HENRY BUNTING.

Bernard Palissy, the Huguenot Potter. By A. E. KEELING.

Brief Description of the Principal Places mentioned in Holy Scripture.

Bulmer's History of Joseph.

Bulmer's History of Moses.

Christianity Compared with Popery : A Lecture.

Death of the Eldest Son (The). By CÆSAR MALAN.

Emily's Lessons ; Chapters in the Life of a Young Christian.

Fragments for Young People.

Freddie Cleminson.

Janie : A Flower from South Africa.

Jesus (History of). For Children. By W. MASON.

Little Nan's Victory. By A. E. COURTENAY.

Martin Luther (The Story of).

Precious Seed, and Little Sowers.

Recollections of Methodist Worthies. Foolscap 8vo, limp cloth.

Sailor's (A) Struggles for Eternal Life.

Saville (Jonathan), Memoirs of. By the Rev. F. A. WEST.

Soon and Safe : A Short Life well Spent.

Sunday Scholar's Guide (The). By the Rev. J. T. BARR.

The Wreck, Rescue, and Massacre : an Account of the Loss of the *Thomas King.*

Will Brown ; or, Saved at the Eleventh Hour. By the Rev. H. BUNTING.

Youthful Sufferer Glorified : A Memorial of Sarah Sands Hay.

Youthful Victor Crowned : A Sketch of Mr. C. JONES.

THE CROWN SERIES. *16mo. Cloth, gilt lettered. Coloured Frontispiece.* PRICE SIXPENCE.

1. A Kiss for a Blow : true Stories about Peace and War for Children.
2. Louis Henrie ; or, The Sister's Promise.
3. The Giants, and How to Fight Them.
4. Robert Dawson ; or, the Brave Spirit.
5. Jane Hudson, the American Girl.
6. The Jewish Twins. By Aunt FRIENDLY.
7. The Book of Beasts. 35 Illust.
8. The Book of Birds. 40 Illust.
9. Proud in Spirit.
10. Althea Norton.
11. Gertrude's Bible Lesson.
12. The Rose in the Desert.
13. The Little Black Hen.
14. Martha's Hymn.
15. Nettie Mathieson.
16. The Prince in Disguise.
17. The Children on the Plains.
18. The Babes in the Basket.

19. Richard Harvey ; or, Taking a Stand.
20. Kitty King : Lessons for Little Girls.
21. Nettie's Mission.
22. Little Margery.
23. Margery's City Home.
24. The Crossing Sweeper.
25. Rosy Conroy's Lessons.
26. Ned Dolan's Garret.
27. Little Henry and his Bearer.
28. The Little Woodman and his Dog.
29. Johnny : Lessons for Little Boys.
30. Pictures and Stories for the Little Ones.
31. A Story of the Sea : and other Incidents.
32. Aunt Lizzie's Talks about Remarkable Fishes. 40 Illusts.
33. Three Little Folks who Mind their own Business ; or, The Bee, the Ant, and the Spider. 25 Illustrations.

The whole of the above thirty-three Sixpenny books are also sold at **Fourpence,** in Enamelled Covers.

PRICE SIXPENCE. *18mo. Cloth, gilt lettered.*

African Girls ; o-, Leaves from the Journal of a Missionary's Widow.

Bunyan (John). The Story of his Life and Work told to Children. By E. M. C.

Celestine ; or, the Blind Woman of the Pastures.

Christ in Passion Week ; or, Our Lord's last Public Visit to Jerusslem.

Crown with Gems (The). A Call to Christian Usefulness.

Fifth of November ; Romish Plotting for Popish Ascendency.

Flower from Feejee. A Memoir of Mary Calvert.

Good Sea Captain (The). Life of Captain Robert Steward.

Grace the Preparation for Glory : Memoir of A. Hill. By Rev. J. RATTENBURY.

Joseph Peters, the Negro Slave.

Hattie and Nancy ; or, the Everlasting Love. A Book for Girls.

Held Down ; or, Why James did Not Prosper.

Matt Stubbs' Dream : A Christmas Story. By M. G. PEARSE.

Michael Faraday. A Book for Boys.

Our Lord's Public Ministry.

Risen Saviour (The).

St. Paul (Life of).

Seed for Waste Corners. By Rev. B. SMITH.

Sorrow on the Sea ; or, the Loss of the *Amazon.*

Street (A) I've Lived in. A Sabbath Morning Scene.

Three Naturalists : Stories of Linnæus, Cuvier, and Buffon.

Young Maid-Servants (A Book for). Gilt Edges.

PRICE FOURPENCE. *Enamelled Covers.*

Precious Seed, and Little Sowers.

Spoiling the Vines.

Rhoda, and Fire in the Soul.

The Fatherly Guide, and Fortune Telling.

Will Brown ; or, Saved at the Eleventh Hour.

Ancass, the Slave Preacher. By the Rev. H. BUNTING.

Bernard Palissy, the Huguenot Potter.

The Story of Martin Luther. By Rev. J. B. NORTON.

Little Nan's Victory.

The whole of the thirty-three books in the Crown Series at Sixpence are sold in Enamelled Covers at FOURPENCE each.

PRICE THREEPENCE. *Enamelled Covers.*

'The Ants' and 'The Conies.'

Concerning Play.

'The Kingly Breaker' and 'Sowing the Seed.'

'The Locusts' and 'The Spiders.'

Hattie and Nancy.

Michael Faraday.

John Bunyan. By E. M. C.

Three Naturalists : Stories of Linnæus, Cuvier, and Buffon.

Celestine ; or, the Blind Woman of the Pastures.

Held Down ; or, Why James didn't Prosper. By Rev. B. SMITH.

The Good Sea Captain. Life of Captain Robert Steward.

PRICE TWOPENCE. *Enamelled Covers.*

1. The Sun of Righteousness.
2. The Light of the World.
3. The Bright and Morning Star.
4. Jesus the Saviour.
5. Jesus the Way.
6. Jesus the Truth.
7. Jesus the Life.
8. Jesus the Vine.
9. The Plant of Renown.
10. Jesus the Shield.
11. Being and Doing Good. By the Rev. J COLWELL.
12. Jessie Allen's Question.
13. Uncle John's Christmas Story.
14. The Pastor and the Schoolmaster.
15. Laura Gaywood.

The above Twopenny Books are also sold in Packets.

Packet No. 1, containing Nos. 1 to 6, Price 1/-

Packet No. 2, containing Nos. 7 to 12, Price 1/-

PRICE ONE PENNY. *New Series. Royal 32mo. With Illustrations.*

1. The Woodman's Daughter. By LILLIE M.
2. The Young Pilgrim : the Story of Louis Jaulmes.
3. Isaac Watkin Lewis : a Life for the Little Ones. By MARK GUY PEARSE.
4. The History of a Green Silk Dress.
5. The Dutch Orphan : Story of John Harmsen.
6. Children Coming to Jesus. By Dr. CROOK.
7. Jesus Blessing the Children. By Dr. CROOK.
8. 'Under Her Wings.' By the Rev. T. CHAMPNESS.
9. 'The Scattered and Peeled Nation': a Word to the Young about the Jews.
10. Jessie Morecambe and Her Playmates.
11. The City of Beautiful People.
12. Ethel and Lily's School Treat. By R. R.

The above twelve books are also sold in a Packet, price 1/-

NEW SERIES OF HALFPENNY BOOKS.

By MARK GUY PEARSE, LILLIE MONTFORT, RUTH ELLIOTT, and others. *Imperial 32mo. 16 pages. With Frontispiece.*

1. The New Scholar.
2. Is it beneath You?
3. James Elliott ; or, the Father's House.
4. Rosa's Christmas Invitations.
5. A Woman's Ornaments.
6. 'Things Seen and Things not Seen.'
7. Will you be the Last?
8. 'After That?'
9. Christmas ; or, the Birthday of Jesus.
10. The School Festival.
11. John's Teachers.
12. Whose Yoke do You Wear?
13. The Sweet Name of Jesus.
14. My Name ; or, How shall I Know?
15. Annie's Conversion.
16. The Covenant Service.
17. The Chat in the Meadow.
18. The Wedding Garment.
19. 'Love Covereth all Sins.'
20. Is Lucy V—— Sincere?
21. He Saves the Lost.
22. The One Way.
23. Nora Grayson's Dream.
24. The Scripture Tickets.
25. 'Almost a Christian.'
26. 'Taken to Jesus.'
27. The New Year ; or, Where shall I Begin?
28. The Book of Remembrance.
29. 'Shall we Meet Beyond the River?'
30. Found after Many Days.
31. Hugh Coventry's Thanksgiving.
32. Our Easter Hymn.
33. 'Eva's New Year's Gift.'
34. Noble Impulses.
35. Old Rosie. By MARK GUY PEARSE.
36. Nellie's Text Book.
37. How Dick Fell out of the Nest.
38. Dick's Kitten.
39. Why Dick Fell into the River.
40. What Dick Did with his Cake.
41. Dick's First Theft.
42. Dick's Revenge.
43. Alone on the Sea.
44. The Wonderful Lamp.
45. Not too Young to Understand.
46. Being a Missionary.
47. Willie Rowland's Decision.
48. 'Can it Mean Me?'
49. A Little Cake.
50. A Little Coat.
51. A Little Cloud.
52. The Two Brothers : Story of a Lie. By MARK GUY PEARSE.

The above Series are also sold in Packets.

Packet No. 1 contains Nos. 1 to 24. Price 1/-
Packet No. 2 contains Nos. 25 to 48. Price 1/-

LONDON:
T. WOOLMER, 2, CASTLE STREET, CITY ROAD, E.C.